MW00623211

TRIGGADALE 3

Elijah R. Freeman

**Lock Down Publications and
Ca$h Presents**
Triggadale 3
A Novel by Elijah R. Freeman

Triggadale 3

Lock Down Publications
Po Box 944
Stockbridge, Ga 30281

Visit our website
www.lockdownpublications.com

Copyright 2020 by Elijah R. Freeman
Triggadale 3

All rights reserved. No part of this book may be
reproduced in any form or by electronic or mechanical means,
including information storage and retrieval systems without
permission in writing from the publisher, except by a reviewer
who may quote brief passages in review.
First Edition August 2019
Printed in the United States of America

*This is a work of fiction. Names, characters, places, and
incidents either are products of the author's imagination or are
used fictitiously. Any similarity to actual events or locales or
persons, living or dead, is entirely coincidental.*

Lock Down Publications
Like our page on Facebook: Lock Down
Publications @
www.facebook.com/lockdownpublications.ldp
Cover design and layout by: **Dynasty Cover Me**
Book interior design by: **Shawn Walker**
Edited by: **Nuel Uyi**

Elijah R. Freeman

Stay Connected with Us!

Text **LOCKDOWN** to 22828 to stay up-to-date with new releases, sneak peaks, contests and more…

Thank you.

Submission Guideline.

Submit the first three chapters of your completed manuscript to ldpsubmissions@gmail.com, subject line: Your book's title. The manuscript must be in a .doc file and sent as an attachment. The document should be in Times New Roman, double-spaced and in size 12 font. Also, provide your synopsis and full contact information. If sending multiple submissions, they must each be in a separate email.

Have a story but no way to send it electronically? You can still submit to LDP/Ca$h Presents. Send in the first three chapters, written or typed, of your completed manuscript to:

LDP: Submissions Dept
Po Box 944
Stockbridge, Ga 30281

DO NOT send original manuscript. Must be a duplicate.

Provide your synopsis and a cover letter containing your full contact information.

Thanks for considering LDP and Ca$h Presents.

Dedication

To my great-grandfather Eugene Hall who instilled the love of reading in me at an early age.

Acknowledgements

First and foremost, all praise due to Allah, without whom none of this would be possible. And STRONGWAY salute to Rich Regardless and Urban Ain't Dead for makin' it happen this year.

5·4·3 Everything!

Monesa, thank you for your unending patience and for holding me down through my struggle. Since Day One you've had my back, front, and my side. My heart is forever yours. You know who I do it for.

Apple Juice, nobody moves these copies on the street like you. The fact that you single-handedly sell out faster in Ohio than my street team down South speaks volumes of your dedication. Love you, Ma.

Shout out to my niggas Renda Da C.E.O, Tavoris "Trey" Jones, Gucci Hudson, Andre "June" Willis, Quamain, Voice The Truth (Juju), Uno, Chris Exom; my cousins Dana, Trese, T, Yaya, Char; my brothers Weezy, Tory, Jaybo; and my lil-big sister Bop for supporting everything I do.

Ambitious Customs (IG: @ambitiouscustoms_promo), good lookin' out on the dope graphics. That "The Future Of Urban Fiction" logo is hard. And special thanks to Telia Williams over at The Urban Hotspot (IG: @theurbanhotspot_), Crystal Alexis at Sizzling Sassy Promo (IG: @sizzlingsassypromos), Reem (IG: @iamreemarkable) and Uniquely Lashay at UCP Promotions (IG: @ucp_promtions. 'Preciate the promo. Real shit.

Shout out to them C.O's that work the hole that be fuckin with the inmates on them extra trays. And to my Convicts #BehindTheWall that work in the kitchen, quit shakin' them mufuckin' spoons in that bitch. Fuck with the struggle.

Big ups to Joe Diamond (IG: @joediamond) for bringing the city together with the #RiverdaleVsEverybody movement. We need to link on the business tip. Get at me, bro.

Much love to DJ Swamp Izzo (IG: @swampizzo), and to everyone who played a part in the success of the world's first ever novel series soundtrack.

Triggadale: Off Safety

I had a blast working on this project, and can't wait to network in the future, as I plan to do Soundtracks to all my future projects. Despite the speedbumps, we made history.

Visit my website (www.Freemanreads.com) today to beat the Soundtrack for free. And don't forget to subscribe to my e-mailing list for notifications of contests, events, and future releases while you're there.

Finally, I would like to say that the purpose of this series is not to promote, nor glorify violence. Based on a true story, it was written in hopes of shedding light to my generation and those that follow that you can't talk your way out of problems you behave yourself into. Also, to pay homage to those who lost their lives and/or sacrificed their freedom to the movements of our childhood, on which we believed to be based on sound principles.

Free HST Black, SSF T-Weezy, N-eze Gottem, Todd Gotti, No-k, B-Smeezee, Takeoff Montana, Lil Chucky, D-Day, Parkway Tay, Bean-Shine, Tookie Gottem, Tray-Day Gottem, Quicksand, E, CG, Bear-Weezy, Rah-Rah, and much Love and Respect to Lil Derrick Gottem.

Welcome Home, my nigga...Stay Focused.

Long Live Blackheart, Rambo Gotti, D-Moss, Trill Gottem, Larry Bishop, Parkway Red, Millionaire Mark, Dyja Harper, Hooride and D-Boi Gottem, SSF Korben, Black Josh, Peek-A-Boo, Tone Gotti, SSM MJ, Cain Gottem

A.K.A Gudda Loc and Rest In Peace to Asha Scott from Pointe South Parkway.

Triggadale Forever!

Growth and change are two different things. Make sure you know the difference.

-     Unknown

Elijah R. Freeman

Prologue

"Squad up!" Sideways yelled into the mic, one hand on the ear of the studio headphones. "Chea!"

He was in the booth at Slim P Productions, a studio on Riverdale Rd., laying his ad-lib vocals for a track he was doing for his upcoming mixtape, "Nightmare On Grove St."

Nodding to the beat just outside the booth was Benzo Gotti, Marko, and Jo-Nate – all three members of Hit Squad Taliban. They had long since set up shop, serving plays from the studio, and they had an agreement with Slim to pay the rent.

Present also was Slim, who bounced to the rhythm of the beat, hyped-up as he sat stationed in front of his Apple Mac Pro.

"Bra, Lit!" he said, adjusting a knob on the M-Audio Interface. "This one gone be a shonuff banger!"

Sideways finished up, and came out shaking his dreads back from his face. "Yea! Yea! I do this shit!"

Marko nodded, passing him a blunt. "I'm tawmbout killin' it, shawdy! You definitely need to make that yo single."

Sideways fired up, making his way to Slim, watching over his shoulder as he did a mild mix down of the track. He inhaled and blew out a cloud of smoke, squinting at the screen. "Maaan, it's a'ight. Depends on how it sounds after Slim mix down 3-Co verse. I just skinned shawdy down for a feature two nights ago."

Benzo looked up from texting. "Who?"

"3-Co," Sideways said. "Fuck with them Benji Family niggas from Y-Town."

Benzo looked at Jo-Nate, who shrugged behind Sideways back.

Benzo shrugged, too. "Never heard of 'em."

"They performed at *Clay Co. Day* in '05 the day before they found Tevo's body in that burned-down ass house on Fitzgerald."

Sideways hit the blunt once more and passed it to Marko, who snatched it mumbling, in playful aggression, "Gimme my goddamn shit."

"Again," Benzo said. "Never heard of 'em."

A loud banging at the front door above caused everyone to look up.

"Police, open up!"

"Oh, shit!" The whole room shouted in unison.

The scene shifted as blunts were snuffed out, and Jo-Nate rushed from the studio room to a back room, where the work was kept. Slim was already flushing the loose zip he was smoking out of, down the toilet in the small bathroom connected to the studio.

"Sideways, get the door!" Marko said. "Don't open it unless they show a search warrant."

"Right!" Sideways shot out the room, headed up the stairs.

"Benzo, hit Kay-Nay and tell him to call that lawyer Brandi talked to and put on reta—"

Boom!

Bwa! *Bwa!* Bwa! *Bwa!*

"The fuck!" Marko said.

Him, Benzo and Slim stared at one another, their expressions the same: a mixture of fear and confusion.

Marko rushed out the room, and turned directly into the barrel of a gun.

Bwa!

Chapter 1

It was a mild day in Jonesboro. Huncho, Rock, and Longway were sitting in Rock's 1972 Cutlass Supreme at the Aquatic Center, waiting for Trigga Mafia to show face. A group of teens walked by, and Huncho – who sat in the passenger seat – watched them proceed to the facility's front entrance. A mother, along with her two small children, both of whom were boys, followed them in, as one of the male teens held the door open for them. Longway, who sat in the back, exhaled a thick cloud of cigarette smoke and tried to pass Huncho a half smoked Newport, which he waved off. He was focused. Rock grabbed it instead.

They were supposed to be meeting with Trigga Mafia to come up with some sort of compromise. Both sides were losing tons of money from war-related loses; left unchecked, the problem could grow to become fatal to both operations. So when Champ took the initiative to reach out to Huncho, he made the executive decision to agree to a meeting on mutually established terms: three affiliates present from each clique, and absolutely no guns, at a secured venue, at 4 p.m. precisely. Any deviation contrary to these terms—and there would be more blood in the streets of Clayton County than the Blade trilogy – which was exactly what Rock Gottem was laying on as he puffed on the Newport short.

His baby brother had been slaughtered – stabbed to death while he choked, lungs screaming for a mercy they never received. Trigga Mafia, the very clique they were there to meet, had left him a lifeless heap in a pool of his own blood on a filthy club floor – one he had been much too young to attend in the first place. He was only fifteen. His mother had been devastated, going as far as swinging on him as if it were he who had done it – he who had always been his brother's keeper. Couldn't she see the tears in his eyes?

Crystal and Tony hadn't taken it well either. First: Flame, now: Thugga. Crystal was back smoking cigarettes, and Tony was on the pipe harder than ever. No, he wasn't with this peace thing at all – far from it.

Huncho received a call and answered on the fourth ring, side eyeing Rock as he conversed on the phone with Trill Gottem, who had been trap-checking on the weed tip. He had long since run dry of the supply he had last copped from the Espinoza Brothers, and was reluctant to deal with Purp, due to the ongoing federal investigation.

And if that wasn't hot enough, he had just been mentioned on the news yesterday when his artist – 3-Co.'s latest collab partner – was found dead along with three others in Slim P Productions studio on The Grove; another was reported to be in critical condition at Grady Memorial Hospital. With Camry three months shy of delivery, he didn't need that heat. Even before Tom and Jerry had advised him against it. Not to mention the fact that he wasn't sure if Purp was to be trusted. Carlos's betrayal had him second guessing everybody. And as he listened to Trill's rundown of some guy he had come across in Atlanta, his instincts had him second guessing Rock's presence at the meeting.

"Bear? Who the f—," Huncho sucked his teeth and looked at his phone incredulously. "Man, you know this nigga?"

Trill gave the rundown on how he had been putting a young nigga – named Redd – from Gresham Road on licks around South Fulton. He would do business with them to gauge the status of the mark. If he felt that the move would prove lucrative, he would turn Redd onto them. He would wipe their nose, and they would buss the spoils down the middle. This was to be the case with Bear, but for some reason Redd wanted to keep him as a plug. At first, Trill had pushed the issue, but in the end he decided to respect Redd's face card. Now with them being assed out on a weed connect, he was glad he had. Besides, he and Redd had continued their operation. Sometimes, with the help of his right hand—a gutta young chick from Hillandale, named Kush, who he met through Rock. He dealt with her from time to time on the whip tip, but she had just been shot at the Shell's on Old National and Pleasant Hill the other day.

As Trill explained how he had come across Bear as a contact, Huncho subtly observed Rock's body language: his right leg was bouncing rapidly, face twisted in the meanest scowl ever – at least by Rock's standard. He was reserved, unaffected by outside influences. Usually, anyways. Something about him didn't seem right. He could see the demon in his eyes, its spirit in his veins, pulsating his temples.

Trill went on explaining Bear's weed prices, which were okay, but not okay enough to serve his clientele at a number they had come to expect, which was sure to create a new business problem in itself. Being his best option, though, he had to run with it – either that, or be dry. He couldn't have that.

"Okay, cool. Just handle it! Know how we do family. 2DM." Huncho hung up and shot Champ a quick text.

Have to reschedule. Urgent family, 9-1-1

"What the—" Huncho sucked his teeth, slamming his fist on the dash above the glove compartment. "Fuck! Ain't no way!"

Longway sat forward. "Wassup!"

Rock's leg stopped bouncing. He was locked in on Huncho.

"They postponed." Huncho ran his hand back, gliding his fingers through his dreads, gripping them tight. He shook his head, feigning frustration.

In disbelief Longway looked from Huncho to Rock, to Huncho again. "Ain't no way! So, they call coppin' duces, set up a meeting, then renege at the last minute?"

Rock's eyes shifted to Longway, weighing his words considerably, before dragging them back to Huncho.

"Pull, Rock," he said. "I ain't finna beat another nigga dead horse, we got enough goin' on as it is."

Rock crunk the car with reluctance as Longway looked around the parking lot, venting about the suspect move he believed Trigga Mafia had just pulled.

"Should slide through Da Joy and go ham on all that fugazey ass suburb shit! Like, real talk. Tryna set a nigga up or sum'? I'm too Southside! I'm tellin' you what I know. Something was just Henry County as a mu'fucka bout the way that shit just played out."

Huncho's phone gave a short buzz as it powered off, his thumb inconspicuously holding down the power button. Rock pulled off without comment, but not without thought. Something was definitely up; of that he was sure.

Chapter 2

Razor stood in the cold steel elevator, facing the wall in handcuffs, on his way to the hole. Behind him were two young black jail guards appointed by the shift sergeant to escort him, having been discovered a liar by a nurse on the Infirmary floor, where he had been faking paralysis since Woadie went up top on him with the mop wringer.

The elevator stopped, its doors sliding apart, at which time he was made to exit, stopping at the Floor 2 entrance sliding doors. The slim brown-skinned officer flashed the floor's booth officers to get their attention, and in mere moments the door was sliding open. They entered, stopping at another door, which only opened once the previous door had slid back shut.

On the floor, all six dorms were on lockdown, which explained its quietness. Yet, only two were actually lockdown dorms: Two-One and Two-Two, the first being the regular hole, and the latter being where Clayton County Detention Center inmates were placed when the regular hole didn't work – *Security*, Razor heard it was called. Through ear hustling, he found out that inmates placed on Security were not allowed roommates, commissary, phone privileges, or visitation, and that they were only allowed out of their cells an hour a day, with waist-chains and ankle shackles; something your average inmate wanted no part in. He wasn't your average inmate, though. He was a rat, and with that fact now exposed, he was in need of a hidey-hole. A very deep one at that.

As he stood outside the booth, he thought in panic of something he could do major enough to land him in Security. He needed to pull a stunt, but like the bitch-ass-nigga he was, he couldn't muster up the guts, fearing what his actions might subject him to while down bad in cuffs. During his first County stint, he witnessed another inmate spit in a guard's face while cuffed. The next thing he spat out were his four fronts. So dorm Two-One he went, through the sliding door, directly to the cell he had been assigned to. He entered, and his mat and storage bin were tossed in behind him. Backing up, he squatted, sticking his wrist out the tray-flap, so they could remove the handcuffs. The bunks were directly ahead and to his right, the stainless steel sink-toilet; a matching steel mirror just above the sink.

On the bottom bunk someone was sleeping facing the wall with his arms in his jumpsuit, making it impossible to tell if he knew him or not. All he could tell was that he was tall, a darker hue of brown, and wasn't rocking dreads with blonde tips. That still didn't mean he couldn't be 2-DUB, but he was locked in now. His best bet was to play it safe on the top bunk until whoever-he-was woke up and revealed enough about himself to be able to gauge his circle. He picked up his mat, laying it out up top as quiet as humanly possible, and slid his grey storage bin under the bottom bunk. Then, without so much as making his bed, he held his breath and hopped up top to begin his wait. On the ceiling above him someone had tagged with a pencil: *Free Da Hole Sity*!

He sucked his teeth. "Stupid ass niggas!"

***

Carlos Espinoza stood gazing out the window of his one-man cell, beyond the chain-link-razor wire-topped fence, into the endless sky of blue. Wispy traces of clouds did little to block the sun, yet the breeze floating past the barred window was cool against his unkempt face. He hadn't shaved in weeks, and as a result, his usual up-kept trim was now a disheveled mess. Appearance was no longer a priority of his. Anyone of his associates outside the Federal Holding Facility, which had been his home for the last two and a half months, would hardly recognize him – if they did at all. A Confidential Informant, he wasn't himself. And as such, he now wore the same stain of dishonor he had made it his business to persecute.

'Blood Traitor,' his grandmother would scream in a rage!

The Espinoza bloodline knew no greater treachery. Things would never be the same.

He trudged to the front of his cell to face himself in the mirror above the porcelain sink. But no matter how he looked in the mirror of truth, he would always see his real reflection. With certainty, whatever there was to see would be nothing short of disappointment; the exact image he knew Ricardo would behold the moment he took the stand. Wouldn't be long now.

The baggy bloodshot eyes of a stranger stared back at him, as his most recent meeting with Agent Smith and Whitfield replayed in his mental, having taken place only thirty minutes prior. They had come to inform him that Grand Jury selection would begin the following Friday, and wanted to remind him of everything at stake if he so happened to get a case of last-minute-cold-feet and switched his story up. And they'd ended the meeting with the introduction of the Witness Protection Program representative assigned to recreate his fraudulent identity, some out-of-shape white guy whom he suspected of being a homosexual.

After a brief rundown of how the program typically operated and a few quick questions, the meeting reached its conclusion. Immediately after the representative made his exit, he informed Smith to find someone else. He wasn't entrusting his life to a faggot; besides, something hadn't seemed quite right about him. His vibe was off. He could be bought—either that, or he was paranoid. It was most definitely a possibility.

Street niggas trusted no one because of the treachery which themselves were capable of. His treacherous ways had him extra conscious of snake-like characteristics. So much so, that every so often, he found himself checking his own grass. A single drop of poison could be deadly. One bite was all it took. The sound of something sliding under his door, followed by something hitting his foot, interrupted his thoughts. He looked down to find an eight by eleven-inch manilla envelope, and shot quickly to the door, peering out its window, finding the tier empty save for the administrative segregation orderly speed walking down the top range.

He looked at the manilla envelope in confusion. He squatted down, picked it up, and stood looking at it front and back for an address, or something that would, at the least, identify the sender, but there was nothing written on it. Seeing this, he reached inside, pulling out several photos: what he saw made him vomit instantly. They were pictures of his slaughtered family, one of which showed his wife with her tongue cut out and stuffed into her throat – a Columbian neck tie, the calling card of the cartel.

He rushed back to the door window in panic, eyes shifting to and fro across the dorm, up and down the range. No one.

He took a step back and slipped in his own vomit, falling hard on his back on the floor. He took another look at the photos, gripping his disheveled mane with his free hand as streams of tears poured from his eyes. He shook his head in disbelief, teeth clenched in agony. Never before had he felt such sorrow. Not one of this magnitude. Anguish swelled in his chest until, unable to hold it in any longer, he released a cry of despair that was heard throughout the entire holding facility.

Elijah R. Freeman

Chapter 3

"Hello?"

"Yo, Dreak! This Huncho. You up?"

Dreak yawned, wiping sleep from his eyes. His longtime girlfriend – Arielle – was still fast asleep to his left. "Y-yea, what's up, bra? I'm up, now."

"I bet you is. Should've been up hours ago. It's 1:35!"

"Fuck outta here!" Dreak shot up, and got his doubt squashed by the digital clock on his stereo, from which still blared the instrumental he figured he must've fell asleep writing to.

"Shiiid, I'm Murk Mob if it ain't."

Dreak stretched. "Well—Whoop-Whoop, then, bra. Its 1:33."

"Boi, stop, lil bra—you already slo—I'm M-O-N till the mufuckin' eezee!" Huncho said. "You need to be worried 'bout these worms you keep missin', Southside. Break-Free shit! We the early birds. If they work hard, we work harder. Feel me?"

"Yea, I hear you, bra. I just been tryna be there for my girl lately. She just lost her cousin. He was one of the ones got murked in that robbery on The Grove a couple days ago."

"Damn, Dreak. Sorry to hear that. It's funny 'cause I think I actually caught that one on the news yesterday."

"Yea." Arielle stirred and Dreak pulled the cover up on her shoulder, and kissed her lightly on the cheek. "But they ain't too many steps ahead, if any at all. I fell asleep just as the dew wet the block. So technically, I beat the worms to the scene. Now, Break-Free that!"

They both burst out laughing at the remark. Huncho couldn't lie, Dreak had wit. Another raindrop in the sea of things he admired about him, which is why he truly believed he could succeed in the music industry – and he would, if he had anything to say about it. All in due time.

Dreak got out of bed and headed to the bathroom.

"Haaa, slo that—slo that," Huncho said. "I got some news for you, though. Ready for it?"

Dreak cut the bathroom faucet on. "Let's get it!"

"This Friday."

"This Friday." Dreak squeezed toothpaste onto his toothbrush, and began brushing his teeth.

"Break-Free, Dreak."

"Bake-fee-Jeek," Dreak mumbled through toothpaste suds.

Huncho paused for effect. "Will be performing his first paid show at The Atrium!"

"Shron Rod!" Dreak said, spraying the bathroom mirror with toothpaste matter.

"What?"

Dreak rinsed his mouth out and spat in the sink. "My bad. I said *On God*!"

"On God, my nigga, you did it! First step in the up-and-up." Huncho released a heavy sigh. "Now you can tell ya girl to quit that job she hates so much. From here, we go nowhere but up."

"Man, Arielle don't care 'bout all that." Dreak washed his face, and turned it left to right to be sure he got everything. "I been tellin' her to quit for years. My baby buckin like a Crime Mob album."

"Yea, well fuck them niggas, too. Far as I'm concerned – We ball!"

"That's real."

"Right. I'm 'bout to gone let you dip, though, lil bra. I gotta check on Camry before I head to Da Dale to link with TD and Jayvo. Just focus on finishing up that mixtape, and try to b—Naw, fuck that—be ready by 9:30 tonight. I'm on my way to meet this graphic designer out in Hampton. Figured I'd snatch up some promo material to go with the free demos I just whipped up at Visions Studio out in Chamblee less than thirty minutes ago. Had them make one thousand copies. We'll pass 'em out tonight to begin building your following as an artist. Sound 'bout right?"

"And some!" Dreak was in disbelief. It was happening.

"Bet! Remember, lil bra, 9:30."

"Fasho."

It was really happening.

***

Huncho walked out of Krogers, bags in hand, having made a quick grocery stop for Camry on his way home. She had left a list on the fridge for him that morning before he left, which somewhat surprised him considering the fact that she hadn't been speaking to him, unless it was absolutely necessary. He hopped in his truck, tossing the groceries into the passenger seat. Cranking up the car, he turned up his favorite track by Dreak, and pulled off out of the parking lot, busting a right onto Old National Highway in deep thought.

He was contemplating Camry's mood ever since he had her administer the lethal injection that left Nard lifeless. She had become distant, reserved; depressed to the point that she began neglecting not only her household duties, but her life outside their home as well. All she seemed to care for now was Zakayla, and the life growing within her. Outside of taking care of them, her daily proclivities were simple: eat, sleep and shower.

Sex was a thing of the past, or so it seemed after having all sexual advances rejected for almost two months now. Going from sexing each other two to three times a day to sudden abstinence, he knew that whatever it was she was feeling, or whatever had been bothering her, was damn serious; one of the reasons he had chosen to be patient with her. The other reason was the health of his unborn seed, which depended on her wellbeing. Memories of his childhood had taught him the dangers of a stressful pregnancy.

He had suffered the pain and disappointment of miscarriage after his mother lost his would-be little sister, while chasing after some no good nigga from the Westside of Atlanta. For four months he had been excited, looking forward to his mother's due date. No more would he be alone in this hate-filled world. Finally, someone who would not only understand his struggle, but share it as well. Then just like that, as if it were never to occur at all, his sibling was gone. Knowing that hurt first-hand, it was the last thing he wished for Zakayla to endure. So, even without being told, he made up for wherever she slacked, praying it was just a phase. More than two whole months later, he was still whispering that same prayer.

Six months into her pregnancy, Camry was an emotional rollercoaster, constantly stressing him about his street dealings. Something she had given a rest until the recent death of Sideways made the news. The confrontation had caused their first argument since the morning he came to her with the idea to kill Nard. He hated arguing, especially with Camry. She was his queen. His world. His everything. Sometimes he hated himself for dragging her into his lifestyle. She was once so green and innocent. That felt like a lifetime ago now.

Turning onto his street in Thornton Woods, the first thing he noticed was Yummy's black Honda Accord curbside in front of his house. He reached his driveway, and turned in thinking about Woadie, who – just one month ago – had his case bounded over from Magistrate to Superior Court at his Preliminary Hearing. He made a mental note to visit him real soon.

Cutting the engine, he grabbed the two Kroger bags off the passenger seat, hopped out absent-mindedly, closing the door behind him, heading inside before realizing he hadn't checked the mail: another thing that had become his responsibility by default to go along with the rest of the list of obligations he had inherited since Camry poisoned Nard.

He checked the mailbox – nothing. Hoping that was a good sign, he headed inside, closing the door behind him. The sounds of Zakayla and Jay's innocent laughter could be heard coming from the backyard, and he followed them, placing the bags on the kitchen counter along the way.

"I'm just worried about him, Cam," he overheard Yummy say to Camry as he approached. They were seated on the love seat in the living room, overlooking the backyard, watching Jay and Zakayla play with the swing set he had bought for her for learning how to spell her name. Her next comment made him pause. "I never told Shoota. Did I ever tell you that?"

Huncho took a step back, hiding behind the wall.

Never told him what, Huncho thought. *I know Yummy ain't play the game foul on my nigga like that.*

Huncho stood behind them, unnoticed, as Yummy used the back of her wrist to wipe away a runaway tear. Camry scooted closer, embracing her best friend, rubbing her back in an attempt to soothe her.

"I should've told him to walk away." Yummy pulled back, shaking her head. She looked out at Jay and Zakayla. "Now my son has to feel that loss for the rest of his life."

"Even if you had, it doesn't mean he would've listened," Camry said. "I couldn't tell you how many times I've told Daldrick the same thing you wish you would've told Shoota and nothing's changed."

Satisfied that he hadn't been hearing what he initially assumed he was, Huncho crept back out the front door. He heard enough nagging involuntarily. He would be damned if he eavesdropped on it.

"Accidents don't make appointments, girl." Yummy took Camry's hand in hers, looking her in the eye. "If I could go back, I'd make him listen. Ask yourself, what you and Daldrick have, is it worth fighting for?"

Chapter 4

Yara was sitting in an Interrogation Room, staring at what she knew to be a two-way mirror-window, through which airport security and Federal Agents were sure to be analyzing her and hoping she would break from hours of hunger. The AC blowing at its highest capacity, she wondered what would become of her. What they didn't know was that she was no rookie, nor was she your average cute face girl. She was a product of Purp, far from green. In fact, the entire Benji Family was well-versed on the tactics of law enforcement agencies. They knew their rights, both state and federal. They were the farthest adjective from *stupid*. Criminals, maybe, but they were no stranger to the Constitution. From inner to outer circle, they were seasoned. Purp had made sure of that.

Federal Agents Smith and Whitfield entered the Observation Room with their short mocha hued translator, Ms. Padron. They were escorted by a security official whose gold name tag pinned to the right side of his chest read: *Gustavo*. He was a big, broad-chest Hispanic man with shoulder-length hair whose strong features gave you the impression he was void of humor.

Smith halted mid-stride, turning to face Gustavo. "How long has she been in there?"

Gustavo's brow creased in confusion, a barely audible growl escaping his chapped lips. Scratching his thick mustache, his eyes shifted from Smith to Whitfield, to their suit-wearing accomplice. "Que?"

Ms. Padron put a small elegant fist to her lips and cleared her throat. *"Cuánto tiempo ha estas alli?"*

Gustavo shrugged with a grunt. *"No cuido niños para los estadounidenses. No we mi problema."*

Eyebrows raised, Ms. Padron looked from Smith to Whitfield before sighing with resignation. "He said he doesn't babysit for Americans. Not his problem."

"Is that right?" Smith looked to Gustavo, whose face remained hard and expressionless. He opened his mouth to speak, but stopped short, catching slight movement in his peripheral. He turned to find that Yara had stood from her seat inside the Interrogation Room, and was approaching the window. He stepped closer to the glass, peering in at her, and could swear she was staring him dead in his eyes. She came to a stop, staring straightforward, as if she could actually see them. "Well who do I need to—"

Boom!

A forty-something-year-old Hispanic man burst through the Observation Room entrance, frowning, flanked by two well-built uniformed officers, stopping directly in front of Smith. "Captain Maldonado. How may I help you, Señor?"

His accent was so thick he might've learned English last week.

Agent Smith smiled and stuck his hand out, ignoring the growing obviousness that he and Whitfield weren't a welcomed presence, for reasons unknown. "Smith. Agent Smith with the Federal Bureau of Investigation."

Captain Maldonado's black beady eyes dropped down to Smith's hand in disgust, before he shook it with reluctance.

Smith looked back, pointing to Whitfield as though the hesitance hadn't even registered. "This is my partner, Agent Whitfield, and Ms. Padron here is our translator. And you are?"

"Head of security." Captain Maldonado cleared his throat. "Now, you have requested to question this woman. Here. In Santo Domingo. About a crime believed to have taken place in your country."

"That's right," Smith said.

Behind Maldonado, his two muscle head cohorts glared at Smith with a mug so menacing, an outsider in passing might assume there existed a long-standing personal vendetta.

"I'm afraid that won't be happening."

Smith was dumbfounded. "Can I—Can I ask why not?"

"No! This country has no extradition treaties with America. I don't owe you an explanation. However, if you must know, nothing was found on her person, or in her luggage. Though I have still yet to be told what my security team was looking for."

"My sincerest apologies, Captain, but the releasing of that information is a call that is beyond me. Due to fear of possibly compromising the investigation, my superiors have ordered all related Intel as restricted information, thereby making it esoteric. Strictly confidential. It's out of my hands."

Captain Maldonado shrugged, waving the matter off in frustration. "Whatever! The sooner you leave, the better. Señor Costolanos is not one I wish to upset."

"I'm sorry, who?"

"Her uncle. He is very much respected here in Santo Domingo, and is en route to this very location as we speak."

Agent Smith was lost for a brief second, in search of his next word. "I'm—I'm not really sure if I fo—"

"My advice to you, Agent, would be to leave at once," Captain Maldonado said, cutting Smith's words short. "Before he arrives. He will not like to find her detained against her will." He nodded towards the two-way glass, where Yara had yet to relent her defiant glare at the translucent glass. "Political ties and such. I'm sure you understand."

But Agent Smith didn't understand. He had read and re-read Yara's entire file, which included an in-depth report of her immediate family, as well as the immediate family members of her mother and father. To his recollection, there had been nothing indicative of political ties. He was sure he would remember if there had been.

Politics was always an important factor, regardless of what country you were in. The rookies at Quantico knew that.

According to the file he had on Yara and her relatives, they seemed to be your average run-of-the-mill citizens. If not, somewhat below average. Farmers for the most part; her uncle, however, was the exception – an Eduardo Costolanos. Of their entire family, he was the only one with a job within the city limits of the country's capital, and that was as nothing more than a basic city cop. He knew plenty of those back home, and not one of them had any political connections. Hell, he doubted most of them voted.

"Of course," Smith replied.

Glancing back at Whitfield, he turned to leave the Observation Room, leaving Yara behind, who was now his only chance of linking Huncho to the Benji Family and Espinoza Brothers' indictment.

He had received word during his flight that Carlos Espinoza had committed suicide. His body was found hanging earlier that afternoon during cell clean out.

Chapter 5

Today had been one of those weird weather days – beginning with grey clouds pouring rain, tricking you into bed ready to lay up in gloom, all to shift without warning into sunny rays, and icy white pillow fluffs. Not even Trello could resist such a spectacular climate. So, feeling ambitious, he decided to go for a cruise. He had a conquest in mind that he had been procrastinating on, putting it off with constant excuses about how busy he was. Not on this glorious day, though.

Today it was off with the television, out of the bed, dressed for success, and on to handle business, remembering a saying his Big Homie Billiano would always spit back home up top.

"There are three kinds of people in this world, Trello. I want you to remember this. You listenin', Twin?" Billiano would say, looking him dead in the eyes. "There are people who watch things happen, people who wonder what happened, and above all, people who make things happen."

He would conclude his message by pointing out that to make things happen was the Blood way. More so was this true for their set, BBA 9-Tre, or to keep it simple: Billy.

So out the door Trello went.

Housing subdivisions, apartment complexes, gas stations and small businesses passed by on either side of the black stretch Hummer H3, as it drove down Mount Zion Parkway. In the back, Trello could smell the pungent stench of opportunity, even with the five percent tint windows up. He nodded absent-mindedly to the sounds of "Hustlerz Ambition," a track on Jeezy's *Recession* album. Doing some major mental numbers, he couldn't help feeling empowered by the events of this year. CNN had announced the presidential candidates for 2008, and one of them just so happened to be a black man!

"Hell yea!" Laughing out loud in his very own obnoxious over-the-top way, he pulled his Blackberry from his front pocket and hit Billiano on speed dial. One moment later, someone answered.

"Waddup, Blood?"

"9 - Shots, Twin," Trello said.

"Tre-Glock. What's poppin'?"

"Nothin' but the money."

"Right, right. That's what's up!"

Trello chuckled. "I'm here."

"Atlanta? Mos def! I been hearin'—"

"Naw, Atlanta been on ball and chain. You got other Blood hoods down here, too, but Billy got the West End, Campbellton, Allen Temple, and Hickory Park on extra smash!"

Billiano paused. "Hold on, Twin. You losin' me."

"Clay Co.!" Trello said. "The next spot on the list. Clayton County. I'm 'bout to paint this shit red. Blatt!"

"Word."

Billiano was above all the Billy's in America, having been made the Godfather over the original BBA line, whose first Godfather got the green light from the West Coast to begin the nation's very first East Coast Blood set. His name rang bells up top. He hadn't been placed in the position he now held by mere happenstance. On the contrary, he had put in mad work in all five boroughs in New York, and in doing so, he had created a reputation to be feared by all. It was no secret. Play with his money, and it was slaughter gang: the end! It was that simple. Recently, his Hispanic suppliers had begun a territory campaign, encouraging their more influential clientele to push down into southern territory.

Following the death of Billiano's brother, Certified, Trello had been crowned Godfather of his own line in Billy – Lambo Gang. Second in charge, he was delegated the responsibility of achieving such conquest. In exchange for territory acquired, he was given sweet numbers on the work tip. The more territory, the sweeter the prices.

"So—Clayton County—" Billiano said. "Okay, cool. Just pulled it up on Google Earth. Consists of quite a few cities, too. Jonesboro, Riverdale, Morrow, Lovejoy, Forest Park, and small parts of Stockbridge, Hampton, Ellenwood, and College Park. Yo kid, sounds like the shit. Handle business, Blood."

"Yo, I got this shit, bro."

The Hummer turned onto Rex Rd.

"Sound 'bout right. How the rest of the homies doin'?"

"They bool," Trello said, replacing the "C" in cool with a "B". Something a lot of East Coast Bloods did in defiance to their Crip rivals. Outside a gas station, was a large crowd of people and a camera crew, leaving him to assume they were shooting a music video. "Hitman still in the County, but he'll be out soon. Driving with suspended license. Nothin' major."

"Cool. And Mecca?"

Trello laughed. "You know, bro. He still bein' him. Typical Mecca."

"Right." Billiano chuckled. "So, when exactly do you plan to set things in motion?"

The Hummer turned into Spivey Crossing Apartments. "Last week." Trello erupted into another fit of laughter. "Robbed a Hit Squad studio trap on Riverdale Rd."

"Yea?"

"Definitely! They never saw it coming. Hit 'em with the Oh-and-wopty."

"5-oh?"

"You know it!"

They laughed again, conversing for a minute or so, more about the cliques that ran Clayton County, and Trello's strategy to overthrow them, ending the call with the understanding that failure wasn't an option. He was to exercise any leverage necessary to the mission's completion. Trello hung up just as the Hummer came to a stop. The divide glass dropped, revealing a fat, black, bald guy in all black with stunna shades.

"We're here." His voice was low and baritone.

Trello popped his door and stepped out the Hummer, taking in the neighborhood.

The sky was clearing up, with the occasional cloud drifting by. Up ahead, sitting on a green box, were some young niggas, some of whom rocked red bandannas. Trello looked up at the ashy brick apartment building he was about to enter, but first he walked down the sidewalk. They were a group of seven, all between the ages of fifteen through seventeen.

"Whaddup, lil' niggas!" Trello greeted them, as he approached.

A skinny, brown-skinned boy with nappy be-bes in his head – wearing worn white ones, blue jeans and a dirty white wife beater with two large holes – stood up from the curb, folding his arms across his chest right over left as Trello drew closer.

Trello stopped right in front of him, and the young thug looked him up and down. "Fuck is you?"

Trello stared for a long minute, before a smile spread across his face. "Who you be?"

***

Beep—Beep—Beep—
Marko was laid up in Grady Memorial Hospital, hooked up to a breathing machine, IV tubes running through his veins, his pain being eased with a steady drip of opiates. The sterile room had been his home for a little over a week now, its pale blue walls and white tile floors encompassing him, as he was forced to relive sounds of the merciless murders of his homeboys. Sideways, Benzo, Jo-Nate and Slim were all dead, and all had been his inner circle since West Clayton Elementary – with the exception of Slim. It was a childhood with memories of which he was now the only one left to recollect—unconsciously.

He had yet to awake from his coma. The pressure from the bullet wound to the eye had caused a concussion, but miraculously, he was still alive.

"Bra, who the fuck, bra?" Brandi was standing over Marko, looking down, slowly shaking her head. "This is just—it's too much."

Meeka rested her temple on Brandi's shoulder, one lone tear cascading down her cheek, as she too looked down on Marko. Present also was Kay-Nay, Frog, and DJ Corleone – T.O Green's younger cousin. At fifteen, he was the youngest active HST affiliate, and never missed a chance to remind the Squad of this fact, boasting that he went harder than many members seven years his senior.

"These niggas got us fucked up!" DJ said. "Pussy-ass niggas done took my niggas' lives. Clapped my nigga! Got 'em laid up in this bitch damn near wasted! Let's ride!"

Brandi sucked her teeth. "On *who*, DJ? We're no closer to figuring out who did this than the police! *We* don't even know—"

"That's bullshit!" he said with a distinct edge to his voice, cutting her off. "You know like I know who pulled this fuck shit! This whole thing got 2-DUB Mafia written all over it. And I ain't lettin' that shit ride. Kay-Nay, is you down?"

Kay-Nay, who had heard the whole robbery himself, wasn't quite convinced of the Mafia's involvement, but wasn't ready to rule them out, either. The robbers were definitely street, but he could tell from their accent that they weren't from Riverdale. "I don't know, bra. I too much don't think them niggas from 'round here. They sounded like some New York niggas."

DJ shrugged. "So! Out of town shooters. They some fuck niggas, but they ain't broke. I'm tellin' you it was them. They been layin' on us since we did that spatula-ass-shit. Who the fuck squash beef?"

"DJ!" Brandi yelled.

"Man, fuck that! Long live Dre and Taliban. "DJ stormed out, slamming the door behind him.

Three days later, the quadruple funerals of Sideways Benzo, Jo-Nate and Slim were held at Hattie G. Memorial Chapel, the same chapel at which Taliban had been laid to rest almost four years ago. With four families present, alongside friends, all of whom gathered together to say goodbye one last time, the sanctuary was packed. Pews flooded, and the parking lot was so crowded that visitors had been left with no choice but to park in surrounding neighborhoods, or the parking lots of nearby businesses. Mourners pulling up to the funeral rode past mourners who approached on foot.

Chapter 6

The room was lit by afternoon sunlight, which shone through the blinds, leaving streaks of sun rays upon the cream walls and tan carpet. 'Four Brothers' was on the television next to the door. Arielle rushed around the room in panic, going through dresser drawers, looking under the bed, and flushing through her bedside nightstand cabinet, before giving up, to wake Dreak.

"Baby—baby, wake up, "Arielle said. "Dreak!"

Dreak stirred on the mattress, pulling the covers over his head, mumbling, "Run that shit back, Dez. I'm finna do my ins and outs."

"Dez?" Arielle jumped on top of Dreak, shaking him with each syllable. *"Dreak-get-up-I-can't-find-my-keys!"*

Dreak shook himself to consciousness, eyes squinting as he tried to sit up. "A'ight, a'ight—chill, girl."

Arielle pushed him back down. "Mmpt! Should've been got up. You heard me." Leaning forward, she kissed him passionately, topping it off with a quick peck on the lips, leaving Dreak all smiles.

"Now—have you seen my keys?"

"Maybe." He winked.

She punched him playfully on his shoulder, making him laugh and raise his arms to defend himself against her next attack if necessary. "Ain't no *maybe*. Where my keys, boy?"

"I'm sayin!" Dreak was still laughing. "I might've happened to see 'em layin' about. What you got for me, though?"

She cocked her fist back and he flinched, laughing even harder now.

"I am so not playin' with you, right now. You gone make me late."

"So." He nipped her chin with his fingertips, and she took off, raining blows on him.

"Boy!"

Dreak balled up, laughing heartily. "Quid pro quo, girl. Goddamn!"

She let up, pushing him in the chest. "Dreak, I swear to God you fuckin' play too much. Come oooon!"

"Yeen answered me yet!" He gripped a handful of ass, and rubbed it through her work pants. "You gone give me some of this when I get back tonight."

She smiled, seductively. "You can get it now if you promise to come straight home after the show tomorrow."

"For some of this?" He was biting his bottom lip, massaging her thighs with both hands." I can't wait to come straight home!"

"Mmm-hmm." Eyes full of lust, she leaned forward to kiss him.

At the sound of a knock, she hopped up with a quickness, out of respect, knowing full well who was on the other side of the door.

Dreak's grandmother – Ms. Louise – walked in wearing a pink and lavender nightgown. "Good mornin', lovebirds."

Arielle stood beside the bed, to Dreak's right.

"Mornin', Grandma!" they said in unison, a little too enthusiastically.

"Mmm-hmm," she said, stale-faced, holding up a sandwich bag full of green nickel sacks of Popcorn Mid.

Astonished, Arielle looked to Dreak, who eyed the bag with contempt before looking up at his grandmother.

"That's a lot of weed, Grandma. When you started smokin'?"

Grandma Louise held a steady gaze. "Jaydreakus Rashad Hart, if you don't get this mess out of my house, boy—I know something." Shaking her head, she tossed it on his bed.

"Yes, ma'am," Dreak said, grabbing the bag and getting up to throw something on.

"And why on Earth are you selling drugs, baby?" she said, the I-thought-I-raised-you-better expression etched across her face; a glare that Dreak couldn't stand being at the receiving end of.

He paused in the middle of shifting through a bottom drawer of his dresser, looking for a pair of socks, releasing a heavy sigh. He hated to be her source of disappointment. "It's not like I'm killin' people or nothin', Grandma. I'm just hustlin' that's all. And it's weed at that!"

"Goddamit, boy, it's illegal! Look what happened to them four boys that made the news the other day. Arielle's cousin! Your mother, your fa—" She caught herself, pursing her lips, eyes blinking rapidly to stop the tears threatening to spill over her cheeks, as her emotions welled up.

Arielle looked uneasy, while Dreak looked away at nothing. His nostrils flared, jaw muscles clenching and unclenching in frustration, as he struggled to get a hold of his emotions. Knowing how sensitive Dreak was about his parents, Arielle took his hand, stroking his fingers with her thumb reassuringly.

Grandma Louise reached in her nightgown and pulled out a green and black key ring, handing it to Arielle, "Here you go, Chile. They were on the side of the dryer."

Arielle grabbed them, smiling bashfully. "Thank you."

"No problem, Suga." She turned back to Dreak, and fixed him with that piercing gaze, that had served as an instant get-right for him since the day he had been dropped off by Children Services, following the death of his parents.

He only saw that face when she was drop-dead serious. "Keep dealing long enough, you'll start shuffling. I've been on this earth fifty-two years, not fifty-two days."

Dreak, who had grown visibly calmer since Arielle had taken his hand, continued to look off.

"Baby—"

Lips bunched, brows creased, Dreak faced his grandmother.

"We'll be alright, you hear," he said to his grandma. "We're going to be okay, just you wait and see."

His grandmother replied, "Don't throw away all that talent that God has blessed you with. The Bible says that there is a way that seemeth right to a man, but its end is death. Be patient, baby." Leaving Dreak staring at the floor, she left, closing the door silently behind her.

Dreak held his gaze steady on the door for a few moments longer, his grandmother's words weighing heavy on his heart. He sighed, and the room seemed to exhale with him. Feeling Arielle's reassuring touch, he looked down at his hand, hers over his, and up into her eyes, conscious of her subtle caress.

A gentle smile crept across her face, and Dreak began to nod, slowly at first, growing more confident in the non-verbal faith Arielle's light brown eyes communicated.

"I'ma head on out. I'm late enough as it is." She stepped closer, kissing him ever so softly, before pulling back to look him in the eye. "You'll be okay?"

Dreak nodded. "Yea. I'm good, Love. I'm focused."

"Okay." Arielle stood and began gathering her things. "I get off at five, but I might put in a lil' overtime to make up for being late. I go on break at one-thirty, though, so I'll be sure to call then. 'Kay?"

Dreak nodded, his expression blank.

Arielle left, leaving him to his thoughts. The weed had been Calvin's – and Calvin was his closest friend. Not wanting his grandmother to feel as though he may be a bad influence, he kept his dispute to himself. Alone in his room now, his focus was on the events that had transpired recently, the most troubling being the death of Thugga Gottem, whom he had never really hung with, but was quite familiar with, all the same.

Growing up in Riverdale, he knew of him and had seen him on several occasions, even before dealing with Huncho. Dead now, life's impermanence truly hit home. Outside of his parents, Thugga was the only person he knew on a personal level to be murdered. He wondered now to himself about the way that seemed right to Thugga Gottem. He had been brought up a Christian since he moved in with his grandmother at the age of seven, but he had always leaned on his own logic. His own way. The path that once upon a time seemed right to him, but now, a route which he questioned. Then suddenly, for no clear reason why, his thoughts shifted to Rock, wondering how he was taking the loss of his brother.

Elijah R. Freeman

Chapter 7

It was pitch-black. Rock was in his room. He lay sprawled out on the floor beside his bed, a picture of Thugga in his left hand, a bottle of Hennessy in his right. He turned the bottle up, taking another swig in his ongoing attempt to numb the vice-like grip that threatened to squeeze and squeeze until his heart burst. His Adam's apple bobbed with every gulp, alcohol burning his throat with each swallow, yet he continued to chug, welcoming the burn as a physical distraction from his mental anguish.

The last drops of alcohol spilled out, some of it running over, trickling down his cheeks. With no more to drown away his sorrow, he flung the bottle at the wall, shattering it on impact. No one was home to hear it, and he honestly could care less if anyone was. He wasn't there mentally. The only thing he considered relevant at the moment was retribution, but he had been ordered to stand down. He just couldn't wrap his mind around the reason why.

How could Huncho disregard such malice, especially when it was Thugga who had been victimized? Thugga, who had looked up to Huncho, idolized him even. His baby brother had been down for whatever, in the name of 2-DUB Mafia, with whoever, for the cause. How could someone's life that literally lived for the proliferation of the movement be murdered in cold blood at war, and die a seemingly meaningless death? It just didn't seem fair to him. Despite all the robbing, shooting, killing, repping and illegalities his brother had committed under the banner of 2DM, all his death had brought about so far was a rest-in-peace track, and a shirt that said "RIP Thugga." What part of the game was that? Wasn't he worth the smoke? And what about himself? At what value was his life held to the Mafia? Or the even better question was, what was his life worth to Huncho? Had he erroneously perceived Huncho's character as genuine, making himself a pawn by default? Surely, Flame would agree with him in his vote to retaliate immediately.

Huncho would've, too, once upon a time, a voice inside his head reasoned. Ironically, the voice was that of Thugga's.

Rock smiled, despite himself, and savored the closeness of his brother in that moment, focusing on the repetition of the statement, until he felt himself begin to nod off.

Even in death you defend his honor, lil bra, he thought, as he stared blankly at the ceiling. *Even despite the fact that he has forbid the team to defend yours.*

His last thought, before he faded, was a mental note to discuss with Huncho some of the thoughts he had that night, and to get him to see that had it been Huncho who was stabbed to death, Thugga would've had zero understanding for the life of his childhood hero. In his mind, Huncho would ponder his words, and seeing them to be nothing short of facts, he would relent on his adamant refusal to pop. Thus, giving the green light to air out everything moving on 11 Stackz. Out cold, he dreamed lofty dreams of home invasions and malicious slayings, in which he saw bloodstained gold flags, and several TMC affiliates that he could remember by face: slumped over, hands tied behind their backs, with bullet holes in their heads where they had been shot execution-style.

A sliver of light touched his face, growing wider, until half the room was illuminated, stopping just short of where the bottle had left a huge dent in the wall beside the small television that sat undisturbed on top of the entertainment system Rock bought from Tony for dirt cheap two days before Thugga got killed.

Crystal had stopped by with Flame's younger brother and sister, hoping their presence could cheer him up as it had done her in the weeks following the loss of Thugga, who had been her closest relative despite their age difference. Standing in the dimly lit hallway, with Rock's door cracked, she could see Rock's smiling expression in the light's slight illumination. Smiling herself, she eased the door back closed, happy to see that her cousin was coming around – even if just in his dreams.

At that very moment, Huncho had just pulled up to South Clayton Recreation Park in Lovejoy, with Jayvo, TD and Longway, pulling up to the basketball court where one lone car awaited. Ron-Meezy, Champ, and Lil Richie were seated in the waiting car. A meeting took place that night, an agreement was made, established by a mutual understanding in regard to gains, and a treaty was set forth, implementing peace on the Southside once again.

"You think we can trust them?" Ron-Meezy sat in the passenger seat, eyes narrowed in suspicion even as he asked the question. He was looking at Champ, who continued to drive, eyes straight ahead as he made a right onto Panhandle Road. "We just left Thugga Gottem the worst way, not even three whole months ago. Wet up, game over. What makes you so sure they ain't tryna play a sucka to catch a sucka?"

Champ, eyes straight ahead, thought in silence, still continuing along the road en route to Tara Glynn to relay the meeting discussion and the terms of the newly established peace treaty to underboss TMC officials. These officials would in turn relay the Intel to their own circles and so forth, until the information was successfully distributed from the highest boss to the lowest peon. Lil Richie sat quietly in the backseat, a clean, all-black Glock 9 on his lap, texting JT about a lick they had been laying on in Hampton.

"Bra!" Ron-Meezy waved his hand inches from Champ's face, snapping him from his daze.

"What!" he barked, not liking to be disturbed in deep thought.

"Answer me, nigga, that's what! I don't care 'bout all that fake rah-rah shit." Ron sat back, twisting one of his thick dreads, fuming. He and Champ were brothers, and were always at it, unlike their youngest brother, Mickey – the coolest of the three. He was always chill.

Champ rolled down the driver side window, and spat as a car passed by, going the opposite direction. "I trust nobody, but I do believe that Huncho himself is for the peace. Besides—" he added, muggin' some M.O.B 23 Hard niggas on the corner of Bonanza as they rode by. One of them, whom he knew as Amp, threw up Murk Mob, to which Lil Richie threw up the M's in response.

"Besides what?" Ron watched the Mob niggas get smaller and smaller in his side mirror.

"That ain't they style."

They arrived in Tara Glynn. Afterward, JT and Lil Richie departed together to hit the lick in question. As were all those previous to this nights caper, it was a success.

The double duo had struck once again.

***

An all-black Monte Carlo slowed down, passing under a street light before pulling curbside in front of an abandoned house in a quiet suburban neighborhood. The driver unlocked the glove compartment and reached in, pulling out a yellow piece of lined paper bearing an address scrawled in black ink. He looked over it and glanced at the mailbox number at the end of the driveway two houses down from the one he now sat in front of.

"Your destination is four yards ahead," the robotic female GPS voice announced.

The driver hit the engine, killing the GPS, and removed a phone from his pocket, before calling a number on his speed dial. Three rings later, someone answered, saying nothing.

"I'm here," the driver said, his heavy accent clearly that of Hispanic descent.

The line was silent for a moment. "You know what to do. Handle business accordingly."

"Si." The driver hung up and grabbed a pair of black gloves from the console.

***

"The end," Mrs. Whitfield said, closing *The Three Little Pigs*. She had just finished reading her daughter her routine bedtime story in her room. Standing from her white bedside rocking chair, she tucked in her precious angel. She had fallen asleep as she read it to her. Kissing her forehead, she cut the night light on, and hit the overhead light on her way out.

She was on her way to her room when she heard a knock at the front door. Stopping in the middle of the hallway, she turned back, heading towards the living room. She passed by the television, shooting a quick glance at the time on the cable box.

It was 9:05.

Roger must've misplaced his key again, she thought, shaking her head with a smile.

She reached the door, looked through the peephole, and her smile faded. Standing under the porch light was a Hispanic man dressed in a FedEx uniform, holding a box.

"Um, yes?" she said.

"Good evening, I have a delivery for a Mr. Roger Whitfield from the Analytical Forensics Association."

"The who?"

"The Analytical Forensics Association. It's a—uhhhh, Federal forensics lab in Lilburn, Georgia. I just need someone to sign for the package and I'll be on my way."

"It's late."

He smiled apologetically. "I know. Sorry. Just doing my job."

She sighed, unlocked the door, and opened it. "What is it? And I have a—"

She stopped talking.

The man was holding a gun.

Chapter 8

Purplish-gray clouds hung low over Highway 285, and the constant fall of steady rain pelted the top of Purp's black Rolls Royce Phantom as he drove, with Yara riding shotgun in the passenger seat. He was in deep thought. Life's recent events had him a little unsure for a while, but having spoken with Yara upon her return, he gave Ricardo a call, and things were looking brighter. All there was to do now was halla at Huncho, who hadn't quite been the easiest person to reach in the last month or so.

His instincts told him he was being avoided, a suspicion he had confessed to his main man and Benji Family Co-Captain, Roscoe, because all the way gutta – it hurt. Why would he of all people mean Huncho any ill intent? He was the one who put him on in the first place. He had given up his personal weed connect out west, and supplied Huncho himself with the best coke prices he was offering anyone, period! Even those who had been on his clientele list for years. Why would he now, suddenly, seek the demise of someone he had only ever wanted to see shine? The authenticity of his character struggled to grasp that. He just kept telling himself that maybe Carlos's treachery had him overthinking to the point of paranoia. All the same, it was all love. Huncho was still his nigga.

At least he knew now that Huncho wasn't snitching. Had his loyalty been compromised, surely he would still be on the scene trying to collect information. The fact that he wasn't said a lot, and at the end of the day, he couldn't blame him for staying out the heat. He had done so quite a few times, which contributed to the very reason he was still free. Longevity was the name of this game. Everyone was just simply tryna make it out.

He pulled his phone out his pocket, and called Huncho for the sixth time within the last hour, only to receive the voicemail once more. Purp ended the call, shaking his head as he turned onto Interstate 10. Thinking outside the box, he scrolled up his contact list and called 3-Co with the intent to have him hit Dreak and somehow finesse his way into his presence, so they could track Huncho down, but to his surprise, he didn't answer either.

Miles away, in an apartment bando in Hickory Park, 3-Co was hog-tied, bound and gagged in a closet.

***

Dreak splashed water in his face from the bathroom sink, and lifted his head to stare at his reflection in the bathroom mirror. His dreads, which now stopped mid-neck, hung freely. He wore a lime-green Pelle Pelle shirt with a yellow line going across the front, navy blue jeans with lime-green and yellow lines running through them, and some all-white low-top Air Force II's. The sound of muffled club music could be heard through the bathroom door, and the stench of liquid soap and cheap cologne filled his nostrils as he struggled to get a hold of himself. So much depended on tonight, and he couldn't afford to blow it. For months, he had been performing on stage for amateur nights at any club he could, but tonight was different. Tonight would be his first paid show.

He stared at himself with disappointment. Here he was in Atlanta, at a popular club on Memorial Drive known as The Atrium, with the task of doing a star-studded performance, but instead, he was panicking with cold feet and a severe case of bubble guts in the club bathroom.

The bathroom door swung open, and the music came blaring in.

"Dreak!" It was Calvin. "Dreak, you in there? You're on in five minutes. Come on, bro."

Dark-skinned and of average height, Calvin rocked a low cut with two parts on the right side of his head. He wore a simple black V-neck with Roca Wear blue jeans and some white, black and blue Jordan 13's.

Dreak glanced at the six stalls behind him through the mirror, as the fleeting thought to hide crossed his mind. He couldn't be seen from the door.

"Dreak?" The door closed, and the club music was muffled once more as Calvin made his way around the wall and over to the sinks. "There you go. I knew I saw you come in here. Yo good hide-and-go-seek playin' ass. W'sup? It's showtime!"

Dreak stood straight. "Maaan."

"What?" Calvin's brows were furrowed in confusion. "W'sup, Dreak?"

Dreak ran his hand down over his face. "I got stage fright."

Calvin burst out laughing. "That was a good one. You hell. Now, come on. Huncho's going ballistic out there. DJ DoIt2eM said you drop in five minutes, ready or not. You've worked too hard and came too far to go out like a sausage. I'll be damned if I let you go out like that. So tighten up! This is that moment Eminem was talkin' 'bout on 'Lose Yourself.' You only got one shot. Don't miss your chance to blow."

Dreak released a heavy sigh. "That's the point. There's too much riding on this. Shit got me nervous as a mufucka."

"Think about Arielle."

"I have."

"Well, think about me."

"I am!"

"Then act like it!" Calvin said, pointing his finger into Dreak's chest. "I put in work, too. It's not just your neck on the line out there. So, come on. Team work makes the dream work, remember?"

Calvin stuck his hand out. Dreak looked down at it, and in it he saw an ultimatum, one that said *do or die*. He looked Calvin in the eye, smiled, and accepted his dap, embracing him in a handshake hug.

"Let's do it, bra."

Calvin pulled back and snapped his fingers. "Fuckin' right! Now, that's what I'm talkin' 'bout. Game time, baby! Wooo!"

They left the bathroom, made their way through the crowded club, and took their place by the booth beside Huncho, TD, Rock, Longway and Trill Gottem. DJ Dolt2eM was on the one's and two's.

"Goddamn, Dreak! Where you been?" Huncho asked.

He had on a fresh "A" fitted hat that he wore over his freshly retwisted dreads that now hung to his ear lobes, a white T-shirt, black Evisu jeans, and crisp cocaine-white Air Force One's.

"Emergency call," Dreak said. "I had to take it."

"Well, take it to the stage and put your game face on. You're up!" Huncho reached back, grabbing a mic from TD, and handed it to Dreak, who nodded and gave the DJ some dap.

"Bet! Say less."

Dreak turned to walk onto stage, but stopped short when Huncho called after him. He turned. "W'sup?"

"Do ya thang." Huncho saluted him.

Dreak nodded, returning the salute, and with a confident smile, he hit the stage. He was a little stiff on the hook, but as he started rapping the first verse he got amp'd. The crowd was hype, and at their apparent acceptance, he turned all the way up. *Tsunami* was the song, and as the hook came in for the third time, the audience began to rap along with him, bringing a proud smile to Huncho's face, and he dapped TD up.

"We on, my nigga!" he shouted above the club noise.

"We been on!" TD replied. "Now, we headed to the top."

"No doubt!"

"Congratulations," a voice said from behind.

Huncho turned around and was shocked to see Purp standing arm-in-arm with Yara, whom, last he heard, had been apprehended by the Feds in Santo Domingo.

"Purp." He was at a loss for words. "What are you—"

"Doing here?" Purp said, cutting him short and finishing his question. "I could ask you the same thing. Long way from the Southside, aint'cha?"

Huncho narrowed his eyes, and seeing how his words had been interpreted, Purp raised his hands. "Peace, brother. I won't insult your intelligence by feigning coincidence, but we needed to talk in person and seeing as how you not only refuse my calls, but refuse to return them as well, I was left with no other choice but to track you down."

"Track me down?"

"Hell yea," Purp said. "You need to know what's goin' on."

Huncho paused, weighing his words. Behind him TD stood on point while Longway, Rock and Trill Gottem continued to converse among themselves.

"A'ight—W'sup?"

Purp spread his arms. "Is a one-on-one conversation too much to ask for? You too much ain't een gotta say shit. I just need you to hear what I have to say."

"Cool."

Purp gave a curt nod, turned to whisper in Yara's ear, and she walked off towards the bar. TD was watching Purp in suspicion. Huncho looked back and nodded, and TD loosened up but kept his eyes trained on them as Huncho moved closer to hear what Purp had to say. They stood face-to-face, at a close but safe distance. Just enough to be audible.

"W'sup?"

"Carlos has been taken care of."

Huncho was taken back, but thought better of showing it. "Okay."

"He committed suicide at the Federal Holding Facility," Purp continued. "Word on the curb is that a small manilla envelope containing pictures of his slaughtered family was found in the cell where he hung himself. I wanna say you can rest easy knowing your loose ends have been clipped, but I already know you're uneasy about me and Yara, and I want you to know I don't blame you. Real shit, I questioned your loyalty the last time we spoke at the studio. Ironically, the fact that you've been dodging me is what cleared you."

"I never needed clearing."

"And neither do I."

Huncho locked him in a piercing gaze. "And her?"

"The Dominican Republic has no extradition treaties with America. She was never interrogated. She's here for a week to handle some things, then she'll be flying back out the country."

"You trust her?"

"Is she still breathing?"

Huncho looked skeptical.

"I love her, but not enough to watch my team fall. Yara, she gutta, yo. Trust and believe. And if that's too far-fetched, then take my word when I say that if that were to ever change, I'd be the first to pull the trigger."

Huncho stared Purp in the eye, and saw the soul of a thoroughbred nigga, self-made in his own right. His word had always been bond. Hell, he brought Huncho to the table. He had mad love for him who had turned him onto a whole new lifestyle. He believed him.

Huncho embraced him in a handshake hug. "You right, my nigga. This shit—it just got a nigga trippin'."

Purp waved it off. "Don't sweat it, G. I know how it is. One thing the game has taught me is, hate it or love it, there will be times of hardship. Along with the ups, come the downs. Even squares have their share of problems. So you know we in for it. Through it all, you just gotta remember that it ain't the load that breaks you down, it's the way you carry it."

Huncho nodded, as the song changed from *Tsunami* to *Madden,* and Dreak's energy went through the club ceiling. As Huncho looked around, throughout the crowd, there was no doubt in his mind that Dreak had what it took.

Behind him Rock was cool on the outside, but on the inside he was in a blind rage. He had just learned through natural conversation with Longway and Trill Gottem that an official peace treaty with Trigga Mafia had been implemented. He was staring at Huncho's back, seeing red.

***

Camry sipped from her mug of hot cocoa and placed it back on her nightstand, beside which was a digital clock that read 11:28. She sighed, wondering why Huncho had yet to call, to at least let her know he was alright.

Is he okay? she thought. *He would've at least sent a text by now. Maybe I should call him.*

Being honest with herself, she knew she hadn't been the easiest person to deal with, but that didn't mean she didn't love him and want him to be safe. That was her issue in the first place: living in constant fear of his safety. If she didn't love him, it wouldn't matter. She would've thought that deductive reasoning would make this evident, but all her inquiries had seemed to get her in the past was nothing but frustration. That was why, these days, she had grown passive when it came to his proclivities. So, she wouldn't call or text him for that matter. But inside of her, she wondered why Huncho couldn't just see that she loved him and saw better in him. Better for him. He had made more than enough money on the streets for them to live comfortably. They didn't have to be rich. She didn't care about all that. As long as they had each other. A tear slid down her cheek, and she wiped it away, wishing he could see that; wishing he felt the same way.

Chapter 9

Federal Agent Smith entered the interrogation room, carrying three manilla envelopes. He didn't know what to expect from this meeting, but Lord knew he needed something. Anything! He could feel the case slipping through his fingertips, and he knew he would never live down the ridicule back at Quantico if he did.

He had been number one during his time at the academy, and made it his self-induced responsibility to make sure everyone at the Federal Training Corps knew it. In doing so, he had been condescending towards many of his peers, most of whom now held various positions within the Bureau themselves. To hear of him being responsible for a stain in the FBI's 98% conviction rate, they couldn't wait!

But they'll never have the satisfaction, he thought.

He placed the manillas on the stainless steel table, and took a seat across from a man he now desperately needed. He was his only hope of indicting both Purp and Huncho, but from the look on his face, it wasn't promising.

He cleared his throat. "Mr. Espinoza."

"Where are my lawyers? "Ricardo asked, eyes narrowed to slits. "I do not wish to speak without them present."

"Understandable," Smith nodded thoughtfully, removing a few documents from the manilla. "How about you just hear me out for a sec, then, huh?"

Seeing where the conversation was headed, Ricardo's face became expressionless. Mistaking it for interest in what he had to say, Smith shot forward with his spill, placing three photos on the table, and spreading them out before him. All three photos were of people Ricardo knew and did business with: Huncho, Purp, and Eduardo Costolanos. Ricardo was curious as to how Smith had managed to catch wind of Eduardo, a man who rarely frequented America.

"These three," he began. "Associates of yours, I believe. These two, I know for sure, but this guy, I'm curious."

Maintaining his cold expression, Ricardo looked down at the photo that Agent Smith was pointing at, briefly, before returning his gaze once again to Smith's eyes.

Smith searched his face for any signs of recognition, but found them void of even the slightest familiarity.

Maybe I'm wrong about him, he thought. *Am I getting that desperate?*

"Look," Smith said, sliding the photo of the Hispanic man back into the manila. "Give me these guys. Johnson and Blanding. Give me enough to convict them, and a little Intel on the Cartel. I can guarantee you walk away from this with a sentence not exceeding ten to twelve, provided you relinquish some of your hidden assets to the United States Supreme Court. I'm sure the Attorney General wouldn't mind accommodating our agreement. It most definitely wouldn't be the first negotiation of its kind. W'da ya say, we got a deal?"

Ricardo stared straight ahead, without so much as batting an eye.

"This is your last shot, Ricardo," Smith added in a desperate attempt to snag a witness. "The evidence we have on you is more than enough to put you away for good. No parole. No deportation. Nada! And with your loved ones lacking U.S citizenship, you'll never see your family again, that's for sure. So you tell me, Mr. Espinoza. It's your call. Who's more important? Two niggas from the hood that you made rich, or your family? They're your responsibility. Not some worthless hooligans you hardly know."

If a muscle twitched in Ricardo's face, Smith had imagined it. Ricardo was 'pressure-proof', and his poker face was impenetrable. It was becoming clear to Agent Smith that the three manillas that rested atop the table, the ones with which he came, would be the only thing he would leave with.

At his realization of this fact, he grew belligerent. "So— exercising our rights, are we?" He began gathering the photos and documents back into their respective manillas. "Nothing wrong with that. May as well practice. You'll have plenty time to exercise a lot more than rights where you're going."

Smith stood, walked out of the interrogation room, and was met by Agent Whitfield, who handed him a mug of fresh coffee.

"How'd it go?" he asked.

Smith took a sip, and cleared his throat. "Not so well."

He began walking. Whitfield followed close behind, curious to know what state his partner's meeting with Ricardo had left their investigation in.

"I mean, what did he say?" he urged on. "Could you read into any comments? Anything off hand?"

"Yea, except he didn't make any comments outside of his curiosity as to the whereabouts of his lawyer." Smith stopped, and punched the wall, drawing a few confused stares.

"Domestic issues," Whitfield offered, to satisfy the inquiring stares of onlookers. "I got him." He threw his arm over Smith's shoulder. "For Christ's sake, Smith. Get it together! We may not have Johnson or this Blanding kid from Riverdale, but look at the bright side. Ricardo's finished. We still won. So what if it wasn't as great a victory as we projected. We caught the big fish, didn't we?"

Agent Smith shrugged him off. "You think this case will be a victory?"

Whitfield stared, undecided.

Smith sighed. "I'll catch up with you later. I need some fresh air."

Smith walked off, leaving Whitfield to pick up what was left of their conversation.

He stood just long enough to watch Smith exit the building's front entrance, before ducking off in a nearby restroom. Nodding at a fellow agent, who was washing his hands, he made his way to an empty stall, pulled out his cell phone and sent off a text:

You're safe.

***

It was the middle of the day, and Camry was at home washing dishes for the first time in weeks. Due to anger and depression, she had been neglecting her household duties, but she needed to do something to take her mind off of the conversation she and Yummy had in her living room a little over a week ago now. The topic had been gnawing at her conscious, and the chores were a much needed distraction that was failing her miserably. No matter how many dishes she washed, how many times she swept, mopped, cooked or wiped down; her thoughts inevitably returned to Huncho.

She needed him out the game. If she lost him to the streets, she didn't think her heart could stand it. She had watched the turmoil Yummy endured following Shoota's death, and it just wasn't something she thought she was built for. Yummy had always been the wild one of their friendship duo, and Camry had always admired her strength and boldness. They were qualities she lacked. But opposites attract, and they balanced each other out. The relationship she shared with Huncho was similar. In him, she found the strength to do things she would've never done on her own. The most recent of which was the taking of someone's life. Never in a million years did she ever think she would've had the guts to ends someone's life, yet she had, and would do so again if it meant saving her family. She had long since come to terms with what she had done, though she knew Huncho thought otherwise. What troubled her was, despite it all, he was at risk, and the solution to end it was still in his power. All he had to do was walk away.

She sighed, placing the last plate in the dish rack beside the kitchen sink. Pulling the stopper to let the dish water drain, she rinsed her hands, dried them off with a dish towel, and retired to her room to lie down. She needed a nap before Zakayla got home from school. The night before, she had been up waiting for Huncho to come home, but ended up dozing off, only to wake up near dawn in a dark room with the television off and Huncho asleep beside her. She wasn't sure when she had dozed off, or what time he had come home for that matter, but she was sure that whatever time it was, it was after midnight. She had half a mind to think he was cheating on her, but she knew him and would sense it if he was. So if nothing else, she was sure he wasn't cheating. So much about him had changed over the years. He definitely wasn't the same Huncho she met at Kendrick Middle School.

As soon as she entered the room, she was reminded by the pictures of them around the room of the good times they shared, and the things they had overcome. There was the picture of them gambling in Vegas on the wall by the master bathroom entrance, directly above the one of them shopping in Cali on Rodeo Drive. The picture that used to sit on the coffee table of her former house—of her, Huncho and Zakayla together smiling in the visitation area at Ware State Prison the week after he received his GED—was up on his side of their dresser. She had been so proud of him.

She lay on her side of the bed, and grabbed her favorite picture of them off her nightstand. It was of them hugged up after a basketball game against Jonesboro Middle School. She was smiling in her cheerleader uniform, and Huncho was standing tall with his arm around her, looking serious in his jersey, his mid neck-length dreads hiding his eyes. She smiled.

Always looking mean, she thought, shaking her head slowly.

Yes, he had definitely come a long way since then. The maturity in the way in which he now carried himself was apparent, but for the life of her she couldn't figure out why he wouldn't let the streets go; though his eyes told her he knew he needed to. She hadn't talked to him about it in a while, but thought to herself that maybe it was time she did. After all, things which mattered most should never be put at the mercy of things which mattered least.

***

"Aye—say, Trustee!" Razor yelled through the crack of his cell door.

His bunkmate was sitting on the bottom bunk, watching him attempt to flag down the floor trustee, a brown-skinned older guy with a bald head. Razor released a heavy sigh, growing frustrated as the trustee continued to sweep the dayroom floor, as though he had heard nothing.

"I know he hear me. I hate when these pussy-ass niggas be actin' like they deaf with that selective-hearing shit." Razor beat on the door. "Aye, man! Brang yo bitch ass here, fuck nigga!"

"Who you callin' a fuck nigga," the trustee snapped!

"Oh, yo bitch ass heard that, though, huh?" Razor said. "Man, pull up real quick, quit playin'. I'm tryna halla at'cha bout some business."

Realizing he had played himself, the trustee swept along the wall until he reached Razor's cell door." What, man? I know you see them people in the booth watching me. You gone get me fucked up!"

Razor sucked his teeth. "Man, nigga, ain't nobody watchin' you! Listen, I got you a bar of Irish Spring and a Sure deodorant for two sack lunches later on. Fuck wit' me."

The trustee looked back at the booth, as he continued to fake-sweep the same area. "I—Maaan, shiiid, say no more. I got'cha."

"Bet!"

The trustee swept on, and Razor turned around and resumed the conversation he'd been having with his bunkmate, a Blood known as Hitman. They had been in the room together now a little over three weeks, and in that time had become cool, both of them being from South Fulton. But while Razor was from Union City, Hitman was from Washington Road.

With nothing better to do, they chopped it up, talking a lot about what they were on in the free world. Having heard no mention of any names in relation to 2DM after their first week in a cell together, Razor grew even more comfortable, but never enough to expose too much for fear that Hitman may catch on that he was a rat. So, on he went about all the gangster shit he had done, and all the work he had put in, which wasn't untrue by a long shot. Razor definitely went hard in the paint. He had robbed, shot, hijacked, kicked doors, and killed, even. His only street-sin was treachery, and when he found the deck stacked against him, he played the police card. Knowing the street life was over for him made him feel like a straight buster, but the more he listened to Hitman talk of his older brother, life as a Blood, their headquarters up top in Harlem, and O.G Billy Trello and his plans to paint the whole Clayton County red, he saw a light of opportunity.

"I'm sayin' though, what's up with that Blood shit?"

"What you mean?" Hitman said.

Razor sat on top of the sink-toilet, placing his feet on the toilet seat. "Like, if I was tryna become official, you could bring me home?"

"I mean, yea. I got the stains to make that happen, yea."

"Stains?"

"You know," Hitman said, making the quote-unquote hand gesture. "Rank."

Razor nodded, contemplating deeply. He figured if he got down with the Bloods, he could get in good with the Godfather by useful knowledge of the Clayton County drug trade, put in work to get his stains up, and start over up top, where no one knew him.

"Shiiid, put me down."

Chapter 10

3-Co woke up in a dark, humid closet, to the sounds of muffled voices coming from somewhere in the apartment where he was being held against his will. He listened intently, wondering what this was all about, as his stomach growled from hunger pains. He was starving, musty, and sweaty, all three major distractions making it hard for him to focus. All he knew was: a day and a half ago, he was unlocking his front door when seven young niggas with red bandannas knocked him unconscious and kidnapped him, bringing him to where he was now. He coughed and wiggled about, trying his best to reposition himself up against the door, so he could better hear what was being said, but there was no use. His heart beat like an 808 in his chest, and his ragged breaths seemed to drown out whatever silence he may have had. It was futile. No sooner had the thought crossed his mind than the closet door opened, and a flashlight was shone in his face, causing him to squint in its brightness.

"Bring him out," he heard someone say.

He heard feet shuffling across the floor, before being hoisted by his arms and legs from the closet, and dropped in the middle of the room. He was still clueless as to what this whole abduction thing was about, but was almost sure he was about to find out. Whoever had just given the order to remove him from the closet was no young nigga, and was obviously the one in charge, the one who had sent for him.

Trello stood over 3-Co with his inner circle of Bloods, and the seven new lil homies that he met in Spivey Crossing Apartments the other day. After the nappy head youngin, who went by the name Wooh, had given the wrong response to his G-Check the day he met the group of seven on the green box, he had played it cool, and finessed them into taking him to their Big Homie, who he dome-called in front of them before making them roll from 5-4 Brim to Billy under his line – Lambo Gang. Their knowledge of Morrow, or Jurrasic Park, as it was called, proved vital. Of the teams and cliques they mentioned trappin' out the area – from Knock Out Squad, to Squad On Deck, Squad 6, Dirt Gang and 2-DUB Mafia – the Mafia appeared to be the biggest lick. So he set out to discover their supplier, a search which led to The Benji Family, who he now needed inside Intel on, if he was to overthrow Purp and shutdown his operation.

"Untie him," Trello said.

The youngins untied 3-Co and stood back. It was dark and raining outside, as Mecca put up a dark-colored sheet to serve as a window curtain while they handled business, whatever that was to be. Trello could be unpredictable at times. He had a habit of being random. Right now, the floor was his.

Trello waited until Mecca finished. "Oh, Mecca."

Mecca cocked his pistol and held it trained on 3-Co, who raised his hands as if to shield himself from the .45 caliber hollow-tip bullets if Mecca so happened to squeeze the trigger.

"Yo, yo, yo, what the fuck man. Hold up!" 3-Co looked frantically around the flashlight-lit room. "I don't een know y'all niggas. You got the wrong man."

Trello laughed. "No! Wait! Please, lookin-ass nigga!"

Mecca shook with anxiousness, his eyes wide with blood thirst. Trello stepped closer to 3-Co and squatted before him, face to face.

"3-Co. Benji Family rap god. Born on Cleveland Avenue in Zone 3, Atlanta. Raised in Clayton County, Riverdale. Brook View, right?

3-Co shook his head. "No, Y-yea. Yea, but—"

Trello chuckled. "Shhh—relax, my man. I just got a few questions I need answered concerning ya boss man, Purp. You fuck with me, I'll fuck with you. Quid pro quo, nah mean?"

"Look, bra, I don't know what you wanna kn—"

"I need answers, accurate answers. You want your life?" Trello was no longer smiling. "So again, quid pro quo."

3-Co's eyes shifted to Mecca, then back to Trello in panic. "Okay, cool. A'ight! A'ight! What you wanna know?"

Trello smiled.

***

It was a sun-kissed Saturday. Ironically, the beautiful weather seemed to mock Rock as he sat rolling a blunt in silence in 5-4-3 Studios, listening as Dreak recorded a track titled *Southside Celebrity*, for his upcoming EP: *I'm Really 4rm Dat Souf*. Present also in the studio was Huncho, TD, Longway, Calvin, Purp, A-R Dreaded from 3rd Degree, and 5-4-3 Studio audio engineer – Dez. Rock still had yet to speak to Huncho about the peace treaty with Trigga Mafia. If anything, he felt like Huncho should've said something to him. He was half wondering if and when Huncho planned to mention it to him. As far as he knew from Longway, the treaty had been in effect for almost two weeks now, and every 2DM official seemed to know the details minus himself.

He hated the ground Huncho walked on. Fuck familism! It was family first in his eyes. What he loathed the most about it all was the fact that he would've thrown it all to the wind for Huncho. What type of honorable structure didn't make exceptions for the sake of loyalty? He wasn't feeling being cliqued up with the Mafia anymore. In his eyes it was *fuck* Southside Mafia! Too bad no one else felt the same way. He had expressed his views to Meechie, questioning how a Gottem could be expendable.

We aint! But you know how that shit go, Meechie Gottem had said. *We gotta focus on the bigger picture, right now. We'll catch up wit' them fuck niggas.*

He went on to explain that if Rock looked at it, all they had done was catch up with them for killing Nard. But that only succeeded in making Rock all the more angrier. His baby brother was as solid as they came. Ain't no way the Mafia figured him a fair swap for a slimy, disloyal, police ass nigga like Nard.

These niggas got me fucked up, Rock thought, as Dreak finished laying down his vocals.

Huncho and Calvin were watching Dez do what he did best, as TD and Longway sat on the long black leather couch, smoking one the strong way.

A-R Dreaded dapped Dreak up, as he came out the booth. "That's him, right there, my nigga. You fye as fuck!"

Dreak nodded, modestly. "Thanks, bra. 'Preciate that, fareal, fareal."

"What you callin' this one, anyways?" Purp asked. "Decided yet?"

"As of now, I was thinkin' something like *I'm Really From Dat South.*"

Purp's eyebrows rose. "As of now?"

"I don't know." Dreak shrugged. "Might change it."

Dreak's phone rang; he pulled it out his pocket, glancing at the screen. "Hold up, I gotta take this."

Dreak stepped outside, and A-R Dreaded walked over to where Longway and TD were, and grabbed a pre-rolled blunt off the coffee table.

Purp approached the equalizers where Dez was tweekin Dreak's vocals, with Huncho and Calvin nodding hard to the beat. Both were watching Dez work over his shoulder.

Purp cleared his throat. "How's it coming?"

"This shit fye!" Huncho turned around and dapped him up. "I got a hell of an artist, but yo engineer is the shit!"

"He know that," Dez said. "That's why I'm here."

Purp laughed. "Yea, I can't een flex, he be doin' his thing."

"Hell yea," Huncho said. "Got me over here taking notes. I might start bringing Calvin through here more often, too, if you don't mind."

Purp sucked his teeth. "Man, quit tryin' me. You know you good. Bring whoever with you whenever you come through. 2DM is family. Ain't that right, Tank?"

Tank had just walked in. "Damn right!"

Clyde followed in behind him. "Say, boss man, 3-Co called. Said he need you to get at him, pronto. Said something about a suit and tie." Clyde shrugged.

Purp looked at Huncho and they laughed, no one noticing Rock Gottem's distant attitude. He was still thinking of his baby brother, as he faced a blunt dolo.

"A'ight, five minutes." Purp still didn't feel comfortable talking in his establishment since the Feds did their sweep. He turned back to Huncho. "Let me grab this right fast. Business and what not. Know how that go."

"Say less," Huncho said. "Take care of that."

They dapped up and Purp dipped, bypassing Dreak on his way out.

"Yo! Gotta dip," Dreak said, popping back in.

Huncho's brow creased in concern. "Everything Mafia?"

"Yea, man. Grandma just keep hittin' me up. I can tell she's worried about me. I don't like her stressin' like that.

So, I'ma take it on in for the night, but I'll make up for the slack first thing in the morning tomorrow at 8 a.m. sharp."

Huncho shook his head, waving the situation off. "Man, don't sweat it, lil bra. I think it's dope that you care enough about your grandmother, to be aware of her feelings and be willing to sacrifice what you want to do to put her at peace. That's real." He looked over to Rock. "Say, Rock. Mind dropping bra off for me?"

So you do know I'm here, he thought, exhaling a thick cloud of smoke, through which he sized Huncho up through narrowed eyes. "Sure. Why, not? Ain't shit else goin' on."

Rock walked out, Dreak looking on after him. He could sense something was up with him. Huncho seemed oblivious.

"A'ight, bra. Rock got'cha. Hold it down." Huncho gave Dreak a farewell tap on the shoulder. "Tell ya grandmother I said hey."

"Bet." Dreak was still looking back at the door out which Rock just left." Everything straight with Rock?"

"Yea, why?" Huncho's expression was that of someone with the impression that they had missed something.

Dreak blinked, and shook it off, figuring that maybe he had simply imagined the tension. "I don't know. I thoug— Nevermind. Probably still fucked up about his brother."

"Oh." Huncho nodded, solemnly. "Yea, that."

"I'm gone, though, shawdy." Dreak gave his trademark two-finger salute, as he back-stepped out the door.

Huncho smiled, returning the gesture. "A'ight, bra. Be safe."

Chapter 11

Rock turned off Highway 85 onto Roundtree Road, quiet, as he had been for the whole ride from 5-4-3 Studios. He hadn't spoken a single word. Dreak now knew the vibe he caught earlier from Rock had been no mistake. He had a great spirit of discernment, and in his heart he knew that something was weighing heavy on his mind.

Staring straight ahead, Rock made a left into Pine Hill and pulled all the way to the back of the apartments, slowing to a stop in the middle of the parking lot, in front of Dreak's building. Making no sudden move to exit the car, Dreak was quiet in thought, drawing Rock's attention.

"You gettin' out or what?"

Dreak looked at him. "Rock—w'sup, bra? You good?"

Rock shrugged. "I've seen better days, but I'll live."

"I understand." Dreak nodded. "You miss your brother, don't you?"

Rock was silent, looking straight ahead. It was obvious that he wasn't going to respond. Dreak decided to let it go. Getting out of the car, he closed the door behind him, and for reasons unknown to himself, he leaned down into the passenger window.

"I ain't get to rock with Thugga like that, but he put on for Da Dale," he said. "Shawdy was goin' ape shit for the city. A real soulja. I'm on this music shit, bra. But whatever you with, I'm with it."

Without another word, Dreak walked inside, leaving Rock to his thoughts. He wondered about the sincerity of Dreak's statement. He didn't even know what he was with himself, so how could Dreak be with whatever? He wondered if Dreak was merely like the rest of them, his former so-called Gottems and Mafiosos, who had shown that they knew nothing of true loyalty. Life had shown him that time was the biggest snitch known to man. Only time would tell. That in mind, he pulled off, thinking of the one person he knew would feel his pain. He needed to talk to him, and when he did, he would go from there.

***

Together with the two Asian strippers he had brought along, Purp stood outside the driver side door of his black Excursion in a secluded spot in the parking lot of Hickory Park. He was waiting for 3-Co to show face with the bread for the four squares he had ducked off. In two separate areas in the apartments, was a tail car for asset protection, one driven by Tank, the other by Clyde. This was a $100,000 play; though 3-Co was family, Purp wasn't slippin'. He had to secure the bag by all means on all plays. Experience had taught him that to deviate from security was to take a loss, and it was too late in the game to be taking losses. He called 3-Co for the third time, and put the phone in the crook of his neck. This time he answered on the fourth ring.

"Hello."

"Yo, Fam! Where you at? It's colder than a bitch out here." Purp blew into his hands and rubbed them together. "Know I got these stripper hoes with me."

A dark-colored Suburban rounded the corner, drawing Purp's attention, but the headlights were on, so he thought nothing of it.

"I see you, Fam. This me in the Suburban pulling up."

Purp breathed a sigh of relief, fully relaxed now. "Cool. Pull into the empty space across from us."

Just as Purp hung up, the sounds of semi-automatic weapons sounded off somewhere within the apartment complex, making him look around in confusion. Two gunshots rang out, causing two quick flashes to be seen within the Suburban. The headlights went out.

"3-Co!" Purp yelled.

A backdoor opened, 3-Co's body was tossed out, and the Suburban tires burned out on the pavement, shooting straight for him. Purp pulled his black 9mm and began bussing through the windshield, but on it came, full speed ahead.

"Oh, shit!" Purp dove out of the way, and the Suburban barely missed him, crashing into the side of the Excursion. The windows shattered, glass littered the ground, and the hood was smoking.

Wooh, Trip and Rightside hopped out the passenger doors and emptied the clips of their automatic weapons into Purp's back as he scrambled to get right, leaving him laid out flat on his stomach. The strippers were in the backseat of the Excursion, screaming. Mecca came out the sunroof with a draco and aired the Excursion out, silencing their screams.

"Come on, foo! Grab the work." Mecca dropped back into the driver seat, and reversed, swerving a hard right.

Rightside, Wooh and Trip snatched the bloody brown paper bags containing the bricks from up under the dead strippers, and ran to the Suburban, hopping in, and Mecca smashed out, barreling towards the exit, fishtailing out the neighborhood onto Delano Road.

At the same time they popped on Purp, two separate groups of Bloods shot up Tank and Clyde where they sat in their cars waiting for Purp's word. Having been put on game by 3-Co about Purp's play routine, Trello was on point about all Benji Family security measures.

Checkmate.

Elijah R. Freeman

Chapter 12

Huncho was laid up with Camry, Zakayla fast asleep on his chest. He had left the studio an hour ago, and decided to chill with his family for the night. On the ride home he phoned Camry ahead, and told her to pick out a movie for them to watch, and he wasn't surprised to see that she had chosen *Kill Bill*, her personal favorite. Before the Nard incident, she was adamant in pressing him to watch it with her. To say tonight's dream-come-true had her in a rare mood would be an understatement. For once in a long time, she opened up.

They discussed Zakayla starting Pre-K next year, boy names, how her pregnancy was going, and finally, Huncho leaving the streets for good.

"I mean I know we've had this conversation before, but I really think you should reconsider, Daldrick." Camry was laid up under him, looking him in his eyes, the glow from the television lighting the room. She took his hand in her own. "I'm serious, bae."

To her surprise, Huncho smiled. "Okay."

"Okay?" Camry sat up, looking down at him. "Daldrick, I am so not playing with you right now. I need you, baby. Kay-Kay needs you." She placed her hand over her protruding stomach. "Our son needs you."

"Baby." Huncho pulled her back down, into his embrace, kissing her lips. "My departure from the game is already in motion. Trust me. I've been hearing you. Just give me some time."

"But every day you're in the streets is like playing Russian roulette with your life. I can't take it! I'm so worried about you, an—"

"Baby, baby—" Huncho put his finger to her lips, quieting her frantic pleas. "If it were that simple to walk away from the streets, on my dead nigga Flame, I woulda been out. I'm tryin'! What you think Break-Free Records is? That's my legitimate exit, Cam. I got a good feeling about this. Dreak is the one, bae."

"But how long will it t—"

"Shhh." Huncho pulled her close, kissing her lightly on her forehead. "Not much longer, baby. Not much longer."

Camry pulled back, looking him in his eyes. "You promise?"

"Yes, bae." Huncho pulled her close, placing his chin atop her head. "I promise."

***

It was a quiet Sunday morning. The sun had just peeked over the horizon to find Dreak alone. He was sitting on a basketball in the middle of the court in Pine Hill, a pen and notepad in hand. He was working on a song for his female fan base, after TD suggested to him the night before that he should make an effort to appeal to a wider audience.

Out of nowhere, someone put their hands over his eyes. "Guess who?"

He smiled and licked his lips. "Hmmm, let me see—One fine cutie with a whole lot of booty."

"Close," the female voice said. Then the mystery woman removed her hands from over his eyes. Dreak looked up at Arielle as she stood over him. She gave him an upside down kiss. "It's your future wifey."

Dreak was still smiling, looking up. "That, too."

"Mmm-hmm." Arielle gave his head a playful push. "Shoulda got it right the first time. What you doing out here so early, bae?"

"Writing another hit."

"Oh, yea?" Arielle sat on his lap, almost making him fall.

"Girl, what the hell! Dreak put his hand on the pavement to keep from falling off the basketball, while Arielle giggled. "Give a nigga a heads-up or something. Know a nigga on a sphere. Shit!"

"Boy, shut up. We good."

Dreak got right, and wrapped his arms around her. "For now, yea. One day we gone be great, baby."

"Can't wait," Arielle said, leaning in to kiss Dreak passionately. She pulled back." So, what you callin' this one?"

"You'll never know."

Arielle's brows creased in confusion. "Why not?"

Dreak laughed. "No, bae. That's the title of the track. *You'll Never Know*. And it just so happens to be about my favorite person in the whole wide world."

"Grandma Louise?"

"Well, I guess it's a tie." Dreak laughed. "But the song is about you, Sweetheart."

Arielle lit up, smiling hard. "Really! Let me hear it, and it better be fye!"

Dreak sucked his teeth, squenching his lips to the side. "Baby, what I dropped that wasn't?"

"Boy, just hit the song."

"A'ight, but I only got a hook and a first verse." Dreak cleared his throat, and started beat boxing. Arielle was nodding with a forced smile, making Dreak laugh. "Girl, you know that beat whack."

"It was—alright."

Dreak smiled. "Awww, you was gone act like you liked it for me." He kissed her on the cheek. "I was just bullshitin'. I'm 'bout to hit this shit for real."

"You play too much,' Arielle said, all smiles.

"I know."

Dreak hit the song, drumming the beat on her thigh, and Arielle loved every second of it. If she was white, her cheeks would've been a hot rosy red, to go along with her pearly white smile that lit up Dreak's world. It was the very attribute that had attracted him to her in the first place. Three years later he was still enjoying being the source of it. So much so that it was literally through her joy that he found his own happiness. His life was not his own to live. His every move was for her betterment, and the well-being of his grandmother. Unlike most people his age, he didn't want to indulge in a lifestyle that would be counteractive to building a solid foundation for them to have what his family before him never had: wealth.

He saw himself being the turning point in his lineage, and didn't plan on leaving his posterity with nothing. His father was a street nigga, and for all he knew, so was the father before him, which communicated to Dreak that obviously what they were doing wasn't working. For the life of him, he couldn't see the logic in following in their footsteps, like most of his generation seemed to be doing. He wasn't going out like that. He was staying down. Music was his thing. The only thing the streets could offer him was generational repetition. So even though he dipped and dabbed in the streets here and there, he maintained a balance, and moved solo.

"Baby, I loved it," Arielle said. "When you gone finish it?"

"Now. That's why I'm out here, crazy girl. Coming out here interrupting me."

Arielle jumped up. "Boy, bye!"

"So you gone now?" Dreak stood up, and grabbed Arielle around her waist from behind. "Come here."

"Nope, I'm leaving you alone so you can finish my song," Arielle said, faking resistance.

"Stop playin'." Dreak pulled her back, locking her in his embrace. "Look, you see that?" Dreak pointed at their apartment building that could be seen down the street through two other apartment buildings. "I'm tryna show you something."

"What, the apartment?" Arielle said, "What about it?"

Dreak kissed her neck. "One day we'll pass by here and say, 'This is the apartment where we used to live.' That's on my folks. Look where we started, verses where we are. I want you to be a part of that. I'm working!"

Sighing, Arielle closed her eyes, relaxing her head back against his "I know, baby—I know."

Dreak picked up the basketball, and they walked home together. They walked through the door to find Grandma Louise shaking her head, watching Fox 5 news, the headline story reading: HOMICIDE - 5 DEAD IN HICKORY PARK.

As the white male reporter talked, live crime scene footage behind him showed a black bullet-riddled Excursion with a huge dent in its side, and a body-shaped chalk line beside it. The screen switched to an all-blue background, showing photos of the victims with their names beside them.

Dreak couldn't believe his eyes. "Ain't no fuckin' way."

Chapter 13

Woadie walked out the front entrance of the dorm, past the booth, and upstairs to the visitation area—a series of cubicles separated by steel walls. Sitting in the seats, inmates could see their visitors through a glass. On both sides was a phone, through which they communicated with their loved ones. All cubicles were occupied as he passed, except for the very last one. On the other side of the glass was Rock. The sight of him made Woadie smile. He was rockin' blue jean Akademiks, a yellow Ralph Lauren Polo shirt, his dreads hanging freely over the collar. Woadie sat down and picked up the receiver.

Rock picked up the receiver on his side of the glass. "Wassup, boi?"

"Shiiid, maintainin'," Woadie said. "You know me."

Rock nodded. "Most definitely."

"Hell yea, though, bra. I'm glad you was able to catch me. I liked to have ended up in the hole a little over a month ago. Caught that pussy ass nigga Razor slippin' and flipped his stupid ass."

"I heard." Rock smiled. "Yo crazy ass. You been the topic in every smoke session in Da Dale. The streets miss you, Wo. What them folks talkin' bout wit'cha, though? I heard you went to your Preliminary Hearing, so I know you got bounded over. They ain't come at you with a plea yet?"

"Not yet."

"How you feel about everything?"

"Optimistic. A nigga really straight, fa'real fa'real. All they got is an anonymous tip from an unknown source. Everything is circumstantial. Back in New Orleans I wouldn't een been bounded over. Georgia laws is fucked up. But I ain't trippin, though." Woadie smiled, pointing at the receiver in his hand, shooting Rock a knowing look. "I ain't did shit no way."

Rock smiled, nodding. "I already slo—Damn, bra. Sorry for this being my first visit. It's just—it's a lot going on out here."

"Like?"

"A lot! Like, a whole lot of sparin' goin' on for the death of my brother."

Woadie was lost. "What you mean?"

Rock mouthed: "Peace treaty! With the goldies."

"The copy cats?"

Rock sqenched his lips to the side, nodding.

"Aint no way!"

"That's what I said, bra. And to be honest, I have no intentions of honoring it."

"Naw?"

"Fuck no! I'm through with 2-DUB and Southside Mafia. I made up my mind last night to push my own shit. Fuck familism. Family first and loyalty over everything."

Woadie stared at him for a moment. "So what we callin the new movement?"

Rock was stunned. "Y-you in?"

"Fuckin' right! Thugga was my right hand. You wasn't the only big brother he had, Rock. I woulda gave anything to have traded places with him. I ain't shit. Ain't gone be shit." Woadie shrugged. "Well, unless you count being a thug ass nigga."

They both laughed.

"Naw, fa'real, though," Woadie said. "What we callin' the new movement, my nigga?"

"Southside Fam." Rock smiled. "Everything brown."

***

Huncho hopped the curb in front of Club 5-4-3, got out his truck, and rushed to the door, hoping with everything in him that the news had made a terrible mistake and Purp was still alive. He could imagine walking into his office, finding him behind his desk smiling with his feet up. They would laugh about how he had staged his own death, and therefore was no longer under investigation. Then he would run it down for him, so that if ever he found himself in a similar situation, he would have that card up his sleeve ready to use it at his disposal.

He arrived at the club entrance and reached for the door knob, but was knocked back by four huge armed security personnel; the one in front drew down on him with a 12 gauge Mossberg pump. He cocked one into the chamber.

"Wo-wo-wow!" Huncho put his hands up in surrender. "Hold up, hold up, what the fuck!"

"You're no longer welcome here," the short stocky security guard holding the pump said. The look on his face matched that of his peers towering ominously behind him.

"Bullshit!" Huncho said. "Says who?"

"Says me." Yara walked through security with her cocaine-white pit bull on a leash, and they stepped aside for her as she made her way forward until she was standing right beside the guard holding Huncho at gun point. Her eyes were bloodshot with bags under them, and for once her face was void of make-up. The very sight of her confirmed his fears, and crushed him in one breath. Purp was gone, and with him, Clyde, Tank, and two innocent females whose only sin was, trying to pay off their college tuition.

"But, why?" Huncho was bewildered. "Yara, what the fuck! What's goin' on? Talk to me."

"Your loyalty is under question and security. The Benji Family is officially disassociating itself with you."

Huncho's face screwed up in disbelief. "For what?"

A tear rolled down her cheek, her face a murderous glare. "For the death of Purp!"

Huncho couldn't believe his ears. "What! Man, ain't no way. Yara, are you fuckin' serious? Purp was like the older brother I never had."

"And this is how you repay him." Yara spat on the concrete in front of Huncho, hardly half an inch from his shoe. "Treachery!"

Huncho took a step back, growing madder at her blatant disrespect. "Man, I don't even know what you talkin' bout!"

"Sure you don't. You didn't trust him. Nor do you trust me. We both know you saw him as a loose end. The only reason you haven't been shot where you stand is because of them." Yara pointed across the street to a white cable van, which couldn't be more obvious that they were an undercover Fed surveillance.

Huncho looked back at it, then faced Yara, nodding. "So that's how it is? You wish death on me without hearing what I have to say?"

Yara held her head high, glaring.

Huncho nodded. "Okay, cool. Say no more."

He walked back to his car, wondering what the encounter meant. Would The Benji Family want smoke? Did this mean war? He hoped not. It was the last thing he needed. With Purp gone, it didn't take much deductive reasoning to understand he had just been bumped up on the Feds' shit list. Not just that; but with Purp gone and Yara looking at him as the culprit, he no longer felt sure she wouldn't work the one with the Feds on him out of spite. He had some decisions to make.

Yara's heart had never before felt such deep seated hatred as it did for Huncho, and as she watched him speed off to God-knew-where, her rage began manifesting a plot for his demise. Just as she had held Purp down in life, she would hold him down in death. She saw no better way to be loyal to his memory than to see to the downfall of the one she felt was responsible for his tragic end, and to continue building his empire. With Purp dead, Roscoe would surely scramble to take the reins of the Benji Family, and for that reason alone she would have to wait before extracting her revenge on Huncho. First, she needed leverage to reason with on her behalf. She had an idea.

"Bo," she said to the body guard who had held Huncho at gunpoint. "Call ahead to the air strip and tell them to fuel the jet. I'm going back to Santo Domingo."

Elijah R. Freeman

Chapter 14

It was early morning. Hitman and Razor stood outside a two-story house in the back of Glynn Addy, where Trello laid his head. Hitman had been released the day before, with an obligation to pay a twenty-five hundred dollar fine. He tapped in with Trello, and received this address. Three hours prior, he had bonded Razor out, with the intentions of putting him through the flame and bringing him home to B-B-A 9-Tre, which had been handled an hour ago.

"You ready?" Hitman stood, poised to knock.

Razor nodded, and Hitman knocked.

"Remember, keep it straight to the point," Hitman said. "Tell him exactly what you told me. Plain and simple."

Razor nodded. He had a busted lip, a swollen eye and a split close to his temple along with a few other minor scratches from being jumped in, but that was the least of his worries. A small price to pay for the reward at the end of the tunnel.

Hitman knocked again, and this time, the peephole darkened.

"Yo!"

The sounds of locks being undone from the other side were heard just before the door swung open to reveal Trello standing tall in the foyer. He was clad in a black V-neck, black Coogi pants, and some black and white slides, with a strap visible on his waistline.

"What's brackin', Blood!" Trello dapped Hitman up, and stepped aside to let him and Razor in. He held his hand out to Razor. "And you must be Razor?"

Razor dapped Trello up. "That's right."

Trello smiled and nodded, closing the door. "Bool, bool. Come in."

Hitman and Razor followed Trello through a dark hallway into the living room, where they took their seats on a couch sitting adjacent to the one Trello sat. To their left was a love seat. The coffee table was in the center of the room. Under which was a cooler filled with ice and an assortment of beer, liquor and wine coolers.

Trello pulled it out. "Thirsty?"

"Hell yea," Hitman said, reaching in for a Corona.

Razor opted for a 211 black can.

Trello laughed. "Not shy, I see."

"Not at all," Razor said, popping the top, turning the can up.

"Fuckin' right!" Trello laughed. "So what's up, dawg? Heard you had some Intel I might wanna hear. Something vital to our operation?"

Hitman nodded. "Dawg from 'round the way. He know Clay Co. like the back of his hand!"

He looked at Razor. "Halla at 'em, Blood."

Razor sat his can on the coffee table, and sat back. "The head of 2-DUB Mafia name is Huncho. That's who runs Clay Co. You want all that Clayton County has to offer, you gotta checkmate him."

They stared at each other for a while and for a moment Razor didn't know what to say or do next, until much to his surprise Trello smiled.

Trello leaned forward, placing his elbows on his knees. "I'm listening."

***

Camry was at Yummy's house, sitting on the living room couch. Yummy sat beside her; ZaKayla and Jay were playing with toys in the middle of the floor. They had been talking for hours on end about clothes, household appliances, dream vacations, and the war that they knew was sure to come, after catching the news of Purp's death on Fox 5 that afternoon. Yummy, who had nothing to worry about besides Camry, was adamant about her safety. If for nothing else, because she still couldn't believe Shoota was gone. She knew first-hand how unpredictable the streets could be. Camry, who had seen too much, knew enough to know that whatever was about to pop would definitely get ugly. She was at Yummy's to drop Zakayla off. She needed her out of the way for what she was about to do. Huncho's time to choose had officially just ran out. She wasn't playing anymore.

"I'm serious, Cam. Be careful."

"I know, girl," Camry said. "Thanks again, by the way. I just don't want to take any chances. It's bad enough I'm carrying."

Yummy put her hand on Camry's thigh. "Camry, I know."

A tear escaped Camry's eye, and she wiped it away. "I'm sorry. I'm—I don't know what's wrong with me. I've been extremely emotional lately." She wiped her eyes, shaking her head. "I'm just so scared for him, Yummy. Every day I live in fear that it may be the first day of the rest of my life without him."

Yummy hugged her, shedding tears of her own. "Oh, Camry." She rubbed her back, trying to calm her.

Camry continued to cry, truly stressed. She was surprised she hadn't miscarried. She shook her head, burying it in Yummy's shoulder. It was a difficult feeling when your heart wouldn't feel what your mind needed it to. Huncho's world was one of pure destruction. It was nothing new. He had been living that lifestyle since she could remember. It was time out for all of that, though. Enough was enough. Their daughter wasn't safe in their own home. How had it come to this? She sighed and pulled back from Yummy's embrace. "I-I have to get going."

"You okay?"

Camry nodded, on the verge of another set of tears. She stood and went in her purse, pulling out a few hundred. "Here, for Kayla."

Yummy folded Camry's hand over the bills, shaking her head slowly. "Camry—I couldn't."

Camry nodded, stuffed the money back in her purse, and kissed Kayla goodbye, before hugging Yummy one more time and making her exit. Back in her car, she sent a "get home quick" text to Huncho, telling him, "Zakayla wasn't moving."

From her kitchen window, Yummy watched Camry back out of her driveway. As Camry pulled off, she said a silent prayer for her best friend. Then, kissing her fingers, she touched the photo of Shoota she held in her hand.

Chapter 15

Rock cut the engine and hopped out his car, making his way to the house of his throwback partna—Duckman. He knocked. It was night out, and as he waited his phone vibrated in his pocket. He pulled it out and looked at the screen to find that he had a text from Huncho for the hundredth time. He made a mental note to change his number real soon. Moments later, Duckman opened the door smiling. He was two or three inches taller than Rock, and his skin tone was a darker hue of brown. He was skinny, rocked a low cut and goatee, and was sporting a tall white T, some blue jeans and some black Deebo's.

"Bwoy, what the fuck goin', foo!" He dapped Rock up. "Come in, nigga. You know you good."

Rock stepped in, closing the door behind him. The smell of fried chicken—and an assortment of other sweet-smelling food—was in the air.

"Mama!"

Ms. Washington came from around the corner, drying her hands on a kitchen cloth. "What boy! Making all that damn n—, Oh hey, Rock."

Rock smiled, giving Ms. Washington a hug. "Hey, Ma."

Ms. Washington was all smiles. Having known Rock since he was nine, when they stayed in Shady Park, she saw him as her very own son. She and his mother used to run together in high school, and had been very close until Thugga's dad had secluded Rock's mother from friends and family. Feeling as though she was letting another nigga come between their friendship, something they promised each other they would never do, Ms. Washington fell back on her. Over time, they grew apart. But whenever Rock and Thugga could get away to come chill with Duckman and Calvin, they were treated like family. As always, it was good to see him.

"So that explains that good food smell I caught a whiff of while coming up the driveway," Rock said.

"Mmm-hmm. You can stay for dinner if you like." Ms. Washington patted him on the back.

"I sure would. Make me a plate." Rock made a head gesture, motioning Duckman to his room.

"Okay, sugar. You know I got you." Ms. Washington made her way back into the kitchen.

Rock and Duckman made their way to his room, and closed the door.

"Where's Calvin?" Rock sat on the end of Duckman's bed.

"I don't know." Duckman sat in a dark green plastic chair, sitting next to the door. He was facing Rock. To their right was a faux-wood dresser, on top of which was a black television." Probably with Dreak somewhere. He won Battleground on 107.9 last week, so they been on the move lately. Then again, he was whippin' something up for TJ last night, so they might be at Korben or Renda's house puttin' something together."

Rock nodded. "That's the move, bra."

"Hell yea, what's up wit'cha, though?"

Rock smiled, screwing his face up in playful offense. "Goddamn, my nigga! I can't slide through and kick it on the strength?"

"Man, watch out, bra. You know you good. I just know yo hot-pocket-chest-ass got something on your mind. The same way you would know if I did. The bond is real. Ya ying?" Duckman busted out laughing, but stopped when he noticed he was doing so alone. "What? I said it wrong or something?"

"Naw, you said it right." Rock's face was void of humor. "I just ain't fuckin with them niggas no more."

Again, Duckman laughed. "Yea-fuckin-right! Since when?"

"Since yesterday." Rock pulled out a brown bandana. "I halla'd at Woadie and he wit' it."

Duckman stared at Rock, taking him in with all seriousness. "Man, what the hell you got goin' on?"

"Nothing but some Fam shit. Some real Fam shit." Rock placed the brown bandana on Duckman's knee. "And that's what we callin' it. That's what it is. Da Fam. We a family."

Duckman eyed the bandana with skepticism. "Da Fam?"

"Yea, my nigga, Da Fam. Southside Fam to be exact, but we on some real live D-A-F-A-M type shit." Rock pulled another brown bandana out his back pocket. "The brown stands for brotherly love. We go hard for this shit, run our sack up and invest. Period! Whether it's in music, publishing, film production, or whatever type of business any Famo wants to try his hand at. If we can dream it, we can do it."

Duckman nodded, listening intently, as Rock continued.

"The Southside as a whole is our Family. We rock with everybody, minus anybody on some sucka shit. One thing, though. Fuck with any one of us from the biggest boss to the smallest peon, we takin' it there. Asap! No matter what we stand to lose or gain. Regardless of who we cool with on the other side. Despite all risks or money loss. Whatever! It's all or nothing with us. And within our structure nobody's above the rim. Feel me?"

Duckman nodded, stroking his goatee.

"Good, 'cause we can't lose. When the ops see how we rockin! They'll migrate. The ones that don't will respect us and want to network. Southern democracy. W'da ya say, you with me?"

Duckman sat, thinking. He knew Rock like he knew the trap lingo, and his gut was telling him he was leaving something out. He stared him dead in the eyes. "This thing with you leaving 2DM—Got anything to do with Thugga?"

"It has everything to do with Thugga!"

"So Southside Fam is just a tool to get your vengeance." Duckman shrugged. "Look Rock, if you got ana with these niggas, I'm wit'cha. But I ain't no pawn, my nigga." Duckman grabbed the bandana and stood.

Rock grabbed his arm, and shook his head. "Woah-woah-woah! D, chill, bra. It ain't een like that."

Duckman pulled his arm free. "It's exactly like that."

Rock stood. "You think I don't know that you with me? That if I was ready to ride, you'd be down? I know that! The same way I know that there's shit you can run on them niggas out there in the streets that you can't run on me, and it's shit I can run on them same niggas that I can't run on you. Southside Fam ain't no fuckin' tool, nigga! We ain't no pawns. It's what I thought I was standing on. Flame. Ski. Shoota. This is what they put me on, growing up on Frontstreet. This is their movement." Rock paused, holding Duckman's gaze in all seriousness. "I'm just pushin' it."

Rock and Duckman stood there for a moment, not really knowing what to say next. Rock wanted to say more, but didn't want to lay it on too thick. His intentions were genuine. He just knew from experience that it was always best to say less than necessary. Otherwise, he'd risk coming off as a fast talker. All the same, what more was there to say? He made his point. Period. He wasn't about to beg anyone to get down with the movement.

"Let me let it marinate," Duckman said. "I'll hit ya."

Rock started to make one last remark, but thought better of it. "A'ight, bra." He dapped Duckman up. "Now, let me go get some of this chicken Ma Dukes got in here."

They shared a laugh, easing the tension, and made their way to the kitchen to eat sumptuously. Halfway through their meals, Calvin, Dreak, TJ, and Korben came in. Rock kicked shit for a minute, then said his farewells, pulling Dreak aside before he made his exit.

"Say, you down to take a ride with me tomorrow?"

Dreak's brow creased in question.

Rock looked him dead on. "For Thugga."

Dreak's eyes narrowed, and Rock gave him a knowing look.

Dreak nodded.

Rock left Helmer Road, not knowing what to make of his linking with Duckman, but he wasn't worried. Dirty rags and money bags was all he needed.

***

"Domonique Carter." It was the booth officer's voice coming through Woadie's cell intercom. He was playing tonk with his bunkmate – a cool white Gangsta Disciple named Spade – on an overturned storage bin.

He drew a card and dropped a spread of Kings. "Yo!"

"You got visitation."

The cell door slid open. From his cell, on top range, he could see Officer Butts pointing behind himself, up toward the visitation area.

"Hold on, shawdy, let me go halla at my folks."

"Cool. I shoulda went ahead and dropped on ya ass," Spade said. "High ass hand. Damn, I was slippin'"

Woadie walked out his cell, buttoning up his red jumpsuit. The bottom range was out on their free time. He walked past two Spade tables to his right, dapping up a guy on the wall phone; he'd known the guy from when he was on the run, ducked off in Newnan. The dorm entrance door was already sliding open as he approached, and he walked straight through, shaking his dreads loose. He walked past the booth, and was about to go up the stairs, but stopped when he saw that it was Huncho who had come to see him.

"Man, fuck naw!" Woadie turned around and made an "X" with his arms, to let the officer know to pop his door so he could lock down. "That shit over wit! Refuse!"

Officer Butts shrugged, and popped the door. Woadie walked back in the door, leaving Huncho confused. He hit the speaker button to address the booth officer.

Beep!

"Yea, man, wassup?"

"What's up with my bro?" Huncho said. "Why you send him back?"

"I didn't. He refused."

"He refused?"

"Yea, man. Sorry you wasted your time."

Huncho didn't believe him, but figured if Woadie had refused, he more than likely had a good reason. But, damn. He had money on the phone, though Woadie had stopped calling. Come to think of it, he hadn't sent a post card, nor had he sent word through Tom and Jerry like he usually would. He left, making a mental note to send him another post card telling him to call, stopping by his lawyers' office to drop some more bread on them for Woadie's case.

Back in his ride, he realized for the first time that he had an-hour-old text from Camry about Zakayla. His heart dropped.

Chapter 16

Huncho whipped into the driveway, parking crooked. The sun was just setting. He hopped out the car, and rushed to the house so fast he forgot to shut the driver side door. He unlocked the front door, and flew up the stairs.

"Cam!" He was climbing the stairs three at a time. "Camry!"

He ran to Zakayla's room and flicked the light on. Everything looked the same from earlier. He rushed back down the dark hallway. Stopping by their bedroom, he hit the light. Nothing.

Huncho looked around, confused. "The fuck!"

He pulled his phone, calling Camry as he descended the stairs. Walking in the kitchen to the refrigerator, he grabbed a two-liter jug of Country Town lemonade, and was on his way to tilt it back, when a sound behind him caused him to jump. He turned, finding Camry sitting at the dining room table with her phone in her lap.

She sent it to voicemail.

Huncho sat the jug down, slowly, his face heavy with skepticism. "Baby, what's wrong? Why you sitting in the dark like this?" He glanced around. "Where's Zakayla?"

"Safe," Camry said. She got up and walked to the living room entrance, facing him.

Huncho recoiled, and narrowed his eyes, sensing the fuck shit that was to come. "Cam, where my daughter at?"

"I told you." Camry shrugged. "Safe. That's all you need to know, right now."

"All I need to know?" Huncho's face screwed up to the tenth power. "Fuck type shit you on, Cam?"

"Some more shit!"

Huncho sucked his teeth, releasing a heavy sigh. "Camry, what the fuuuck! Come on, now. I ain't got time for this. What's this shit about?"

"Everything, Daldrick!" Camry screamed. "I did something I never imagined I would ever have to do today. Take a guess."

Huncho pinched the bridge of his nose. "Camry, please. I rea—"

Camry rushed him, putting her finger in his chest. "Don't you dare! Don't fuckin' Camry, Please! Me!"

He put his arm out to keep her at a distance, but she slapped it away, jumped in his face, and jammed her finger in his cheek. "You got some damn nerves. You need to grow the fuck up, Daldrick! You're not seventeen anymore. You have a fuckin' family."

Huncho had his head turned as she continued to poke his face, screaming like a mad woman.

Camry grabbed his face and snatched him, making him face her. "Look at me!"
Huncho looked into her eyes as they welled up with tears. Feeling his heart twitch, he shifted his gaze. She yanked his head back to face her.

"So that's how you feel?" She stared at him, his head still in her hand. "Daldrick!"

"What!" Huncho snatched away from her, and made his way to the door.

Camry was on his heels. "Say something!"

"I don't know what you want me to say." He reached for the door knob. "I'm still tryna figure out where my daughter at."

Camry put her weight on the door, and locked it. Huncho sucked his teeth. "Maaan. Camry, watch out, now." She didn't budge. "Get the fuck out the way, Cam, damn!"

"Nigga!" Camry swung punches of fury, the first three catching him dead in the nose and mouth. "I'm tired of you tryin' me!"

Huncho struggled to get ahold of her arms. "C-Cam!" She landed one to his eye. He grabbed that arm, and she kneed him, missing a head butt. "Cam, what the fuck!"

"No!" She rushed him, knocking down pictures from the living room coffee table. "Let me go! Daldrick, I swear to fuckin' God! Get your hands off me. Now!"

"Calm yo ass down, then." They fell to the floor, wrestling. "Camry, chill! You pregnant!"

"Glad you finally noticed." She struggled to free herself from his gasp, but it was futile. "I fuckin' hate you! You don't give a fuck about us. All you care about is the streets. That's all you ever cared about."

"I don't hear you complainin' when a nigga lacin' you in designer."

"Designer? You think I—" Camry bit Huncho's hand, clamping down with all her might.

"Argh, shit! What the fuck!"

Camry broke away and ran for the stairs. "I'ma sho yo ass tonight."

Huncho got up just in time to see her disappear up the stairs. "Camry!" He rushed behind her, shaking his hand, trying to ease the pain as he climbed the stairs. "Camry!"

He could hear her ranting and raving as she ran around their bedroom. The closer he got to the room, he heard the sound of liquid splashing. He made it to the bedroom, and what he saw put him in a state of alarm. He raised both hands, willing her to go no further. "Camry, stop fuckin' playin', a'ight? Put that shit down."

She had poured rubbing alcohol on the clothes hanging in the closet, and now stood with a lit match at its entrance.

Fuck you, Daldrick! I ain't puttin' shit down. You think I cherish this shit over you?" She had the match pointed back at the closet. "Over our babies?"

"Naw, baby. Just, please put the match down, Cam. Please!" Huncho realized he had pushed her over the edge. The crazed look in her eyes. The ever flowing tears. Her disheveled hair. She wasn't in her right mind.

She let out a laugh straight from the psych ward. "I guess someone does—I don't." She tossed the match in the back of the closet.

"No!" Huncho started in after it, but stopped as the heat burst from the instant flames. "Fuck!" He grabbed her by the shoulders, shaking. "Are you fuckin' crazy!"

"You fuckin' right I am, Daldrick! Out my fucking mind!" She swung, but he ducked, backing up. "I took someone's life for you! You ungrateful—" Swinging in a rage, she charged at him, but slipped and fell, hitting her head on the dresser. She was out cold.

"Shit! Shit! Shit! Shit! Shit!" Huncho got down, and listened for breathing.

She was breathing.

He looked at the closet. Thick dark clouds of smoke were billowing from the top of the door frame, and suddenly, he was overcome with a strange calm. He was tripping. None of this shit meant more than his family. Not the sound system, the eighty-two inch flat, the California king size bed, not even the racks he had hidden in the closet, trapped now to be consumed by the raging fire.

He looked down at Camry, who was lying unconscious on the floor. Reaching down, he lifted her, deciding to leave the house to ruin. To hell with it.

As he descended the stairs he planted a kiss on Camry's cheeks.

"You right, bae." He walked out the front door. "Fuck this house."

***

The smell of fresh paint filled the air. All drawers, cabinets, and closets, were bare; all carpets and paddings ripped up and gone. Even the tub and toilet bowl stains had been removed. No dust, cobwebs, or dirt under the kitchen sink. The place was sterile. Every room had a fresh coat of dull white, except the living room, which was half-finished and where the first B-B-A 9-Tre Blood Gang meeting was being held, with Trello presiding. Around him stood approximately one hundred bloods draped in red, rocking red bandannas in various ways, the most common of which was out their back right pocket. Standing closest was Razor, Mecca, Wooh, Rightside, Hitman, and Trip.

Everyone had shown up to hear the breakdown of the structure and the rundown of the game plan. Up until now, they had free-styled, but they were determined to chart a new course henceforth. The history of the Blood Gang's move from the West coast to the East coast had demonstrated that, sooner or later, they would need to strategize and go in for the kill, all gas and no breaks. Trello wasn't new to this; he was true to this, and felt that now was the time to delegate positions. Now was the time to discuss methods and tactics. Now was the time for a hostile takeover.

"I brought you bros here today," Trello began, "because it's our time. From this day forward, we all in. No games! As we demonstrated in this very neighborhood just last week, we takin' the Southside by storm. I have in here among us Billy bros from Campbellton, the West End, various hoods throughout Atlanta, and of course, from right here in Hickory Park."

The room erupted in cheers of "Blatts" and "Whoops."

"We got eight official homies within our ranks from Clayton County who fuckin' with us on some inside Intel to speed this thing up. One of 'em got their first stripes last week with his hand in the demise of Benji Family head, Purp, and their star artist, 3-Co. This young homie here will be the future face of Lambo Gang Records." Trello took a few steps to his right, and put his hand on Wooh's shoulder. "Wooh!"

More cheers erupted, and at this, Wooh grinned arrogantly. A homie to his left showed him some Blood love, dapping him up with the Blood handshake.

"Young Wooh here ain't nothin' but sixteen, and already, his future in the Blood Gang is looking promising. Not only has he shed blood for the cause, but he's young and ambitious. Y'all older bros who want stains, tighten up."

Razor nodded, hanging on his every word.

"Now, before I continue," Trello said, "I want everyone to welcome home the lil-big homie, Hitman."

"Blatt! Blatt!" Multiple homies showed their love and appreciation for Hitman's return to the scene. He had mad love and respect from the gang. He smiled as he received claps, salutes, and pats on the back from homies all around. Mecca simply stood stone-faced, arms folded across his chest. He sucked his teeth, releasing a heavy sigh as Trello continued.

"As some of you may already know, the first five floors of this bloodline have been established, with the Low and High open, which I have decided. Our low." Trello pointed at Mecca, who stood posted indifferently. "Mecca!"

Mecca's eyes narrowed as cheers erupted around him.

"Our high." Trello pointed to Hitman. "Hitman!"

More cheers sounded off, even louder, and Mecca gritted his teeth, glaring at Trello, then Hitman.

"Settle down," Trello said, waving them down. "Now listen, every homie with the GL, put your scraps to work. Press game one million on everything that ain't bangin' red. If your scrap game low, get to breedin'. Every hood with a trap, they either line up, or get shut the fuck down! Whoop?"

"Whoop!" the room erupted in unison.

Trello continued. Mecca slid back through the crowd and slipped out the front door. He needed to smoke one after that. There was no way Hitman had made the High over him. He was a Lambo Gang original, and before that he had been under the same line that originally brought Trello home. Before he was made Godfather of his very own: Strongwhip, the line that was headed by Certified, Billiano's younger brother. He was dead now. Had been for a little over a year now. Mecca pulled a pack of Newports from his pocket, removed a single from the box, and fired it up. He took a pull and exhaled, thinking of how it was the work he put in that got Trello his position in the first place. He felt he deserved the post of High, and was mad that Trello hadn't given him his just dues. He earned those stains. The fact that it seemed Trello had forgot was a problem. He would be sure to remind him. And soon.

Inside the apartment, Trello went on. "Pretty soon we'll be moving in on 2DM. They control most of the trap trade on the Southside, and right now they're in the way of what we tryna do. So they gotta go. The organization is headed by a nigga named Huncho, who as of right now is officially a plate. I got fifty K and the position as First Floor to whoever eat him. Any volunteers?"

Elijah R. Freeman

Chapter 17

Special Agent Whitfield pulled into the parking lot of an abandoned warehouse, slowing to a stop at its center. Hands shaking, he pulled out his phone, calling the number he had been given to call once he reached his current location. The line rang six times before going to voicemail. He called back, only to get the same result.

"Come on," Whitfield said, sweating profusely. "Answer me!"

He wiped sweat from his brow with the cuff of his suit, and glanced around the deserted lot. None of the overhead lights were on, giving the lot a barren look. The paint lines of the parking spaces were faded, the concrete was cracked, and weeds had begun to sprout here and there throughout the wide open space. He tried the number once more. Nothing.

"Please," he gasped.

His phone vibrated, indicating an incoming text from the number he had just called.

Drive around to the back.

Whitfield glanced around once more, put his car in drive, and pulled around to the back, cutting the headlights. He was growing more nervous by the minute. He texted back:

What now?

Moments later, a flashlight flicked on and off in a window. He began a text, but stopped when another message came through.

Come in. And bring the documents.

Whitfield wiped his brow once more, and cut his engine. Gathering the documents up from the passenger seat, he got out the car, closed the door behind him and hurried to the back entrance of the warehouse, which had been left ajar. He pushed it open, peering inside, but it was much too dark to see more than a few feet in front of him into the shadows. He hesitated, but threw caution to the wind. He was on a mission, and a detrimental one at that. Nothing else would matter if the mission turned out to be a failure. His wife and daughter had been kidnapped by someone who claimed to be moving on behalf of Ricardo Espinoza, and had made his demands clear. He wanted Intel on any low-key informants, a full coverage file on the judge handling his case, and email access codes to a few choice federal agents.

In exchange for the documents and his word to continue to work for them as an inside job, his loved ones would be set free. But if he tried pulling a stunt, he and his family would be tracked down and murdered mercilessly. He was at the warehouse to make the swap. The documents in exchange for his family. He was there to meet Dinero.

***

Rock closed the driver side door and followed Duckman to the backyard of the white two-floor house they were parked out front of, curbside. They were in Elon Farm, off Pointe South Parkway, to meet with Burnout and a few others. Duckman had called Rock the morning after he paid him a visit, to tell him he was with the movement, and that TJ, Calvin, Renda, and the whole Helmer Road was in as well. It was official. Helmer Road was the home of Da Fam, and they were calling it 1100 Block.

It was TJ's suggestion that they clique up with Murk Mob, who just so happened to be cliqued up with M.O.B 23, known to be bitter enemies of Trigga Mafia and 2DM. Rock didn't like the idea, but had never heard of them going out bad or leaving one of their own in the water, so he was down with it for territory purposes. Though there was a long standing relationship between 1100 Block and Da Parkway, the idea was to lock Clayton County down from Helmer Road to Bonanza, which consisted of three cities. Riverdale, Jonesboro, and Lovejoy.

They jumped the fence, and four niggas on the back porch hopped up with straps—the tallest of whom was toting a choppa.

Duckman and Rock threw their hands up in surrender.

"Woah-woah, chill, bra," Duckman said. "It's me, Duckman."

They lowered their weapons.

"Boy, Duckman, you liked to just got yo ass bussed." Burnout dapped Duckman up when he reached the porch.

Burnout was of average height, had dark, curly hair, hazel eyes that he inherited from his Puerto Rican mother, and skin the color of beach sand. "I ain't gone say too much, but TMC Lil Richie got handled last night, so we extra on point. Who this?"

"This my nigga, Rock, TJ was tellin' you bout."

"Oh yea, Southside Fam. Waddup, my nigga?" He dapped Rock up. "They call me Burnout."

"Fashow."

He turned around and pointed at the tall, lanky, nappy head brown-skinned guy holding the choppa. "That's Hot-Deezy. He Mob." He nodded back at the two niggas behind him. "That's Rio and Dec. They just Parkway."

Rock dapped them both up. "What's up bra? Whaddup?"

Rio shook his dreads back out of his face, squinted at him, and scratched his head with his .45. "Yo, ain't you 2-DUB?"

"Fuck Da Dub!"

Rio looked to Burnout, who shrugged, pulled out a box of Newports, and removed a single. Dec was clutchin' and Rock peeped the move.

He put his hand on his waist. "It's a problem?"

Dec drew down on him with his black 9mm. "Yea, nigga. I don't trust yo mufuckin ass!"

Rock up'd his strap. "Fuck you, nigga. Ain't shit cutthroat bout Rock. If I said it, then I meant it. Trust that, or trust some hot bullets."

Hot-Deezy and Rio took aim at Rock.

"Hold up, Dec." Burnout put his hand on Dec's strap and lowered his weapon. "TJ and Duckman say he good, he good."

Rock lowered his weapon. Duckman stepped in between them. Hot-Deezy lowered the choppa. Rio tucked his burner back on his waistline.

"Duckman, what makes you so sure we can trust him? Better yet, tell us, Rock! Why the change of heart?" Dec spat in the grass. "How we know you genuine? This could be a set-up."

"Who you ever known me to cross?"

"You crossin' them now! Rio said.

Rock pointed behind himself. "They crossed me first when they made a treaty with the fuck niggas who killed my lil brother. Where the fuck they do that at, huh? That sound like some loyal shit to you? Fuck no! I realized I was playin' for the wrong team, so I started my own movement, not switch sides." He pointed at Duckman. "He's the reason I'm here, but I could give a fuck 'bout it. All I know is, y'all stand up for y'all own. That's solid. But make no mistake, I don't need nan nigga to ride for me. I'm too official. Now, is y'all tryna make some money or what?"

Rio, Hot-Deezy, and Burnout looked at Dec, who seemed to have calmed down a little.

"Hey, how bout we take this thing back a few steps," Burnout said.

"Yea man," Duckman said. "Me and bra go back to Shady Park. He wouldn't e'en try my face card like that. And you got to know if me and TJ vouched for him, he good."

Dec shook his head. "Naw, Duckman, you straight, but I done seen too much out here in these streets. That's how A-Jeezy got killed. Ya boy gone have to show us something."

"Dec, man—"

"Fuck that," Rock said, cutting Duckman off. "You want me to show you I'm serious? That's real." He tapped Duckman on the arm. "Let's ride."

Rock turned around. "Ya boy wanna see something. I gottem. We'll be in touch."

Rock and Duckman hopped back over the fence, walked to the car, and got in.

"So, what now?" Duckman said.

Rock started the car. "Shiiid, what else? We make some examples!"

Rock pulled off, and made a phone call to one of his throwback partnas from Lake Ridge. He answered as he made a right onto Pointe South Parkway.

"Talk."

"Aye Quamain, this Rock. You in the hood?"

"You know it!"

"Be on standby. I'm pullin' up."

Chapter 18

Huncho was tucked away safely in the calm suburban streets of Villa Rica, Georgia, under the name Tyrone Curtis. A couple weeks had shot by, and he and his family had gone from staying in the Marriott, to his new residence, a gated community called The Fairfield Plantation, far removed from the reaches of Riverdale. In his absence, TD had been in charge of the Mafia's affairs. Surprisingly, things had been quiet since the murders of Purp and 3-Co. He still couldn't believe they were gone, and wanted – with everything in him – to track down the fuck niggas responsible for their death.

The only problem was, he had no idea where to start. Word on the curb was that he himself had slimed them out, so he knew the streets were not a creditable source. He knew for a fact he had nothing to do with it, which was what made the hit so puzzling. Nothing had surfaced with regard to their mysterious murders, which led Huncho to believe that whoever actually was behind it wasn't from here. The only reason he was a suspect to the streets was owing to deductive reasoning, and the fact that both he and Purp had been targets of the same federal investigation, a case which – according to his lawyer – had gone cold with the death of Special Agent Whitfield. He, with his wife and daughter, had been found dead in a warehouse. The only one still facing criminal charges was Ricardo Espinoza, who had just been indicted the day before. His court date had been pushed back after Carlos's suicide. Let Tom and Jerry tell it, he had absolutely nothing to worry about as far as an indictment was concerned. From here on out he need only play it safe. Camry's episode had been perfect timing.

To keep her happy, he had stuck around the house, returning to Riverdale once or twice to show face, and check the trap. All was well, but the one thing that struck him as odd was no one in 2-DUB or the Mafia had seen Rock or heard from him. He tried calling, but his number had been changed, so he stopped by his house on Scott Road. Nothing, still. On top of that, he had sent Woadie a post card, telling him to reach out to him, and sent word through Tom and Jerry, but he had yet to call. Being out of sync with the streets had him in the blind. The closest his ear had been to the block, outside of the couple of trips he made to Riverdale, was the string of conversations he had with Dreak, which had been very few.

He had mentioned running into Rock a week ago on Helmer Road. They were supposed to have linked up the following night; but, according to Dreak, he called and cancelled that afternoon for some reason unbeknownst to him. Huncho shook his head, thinking that with everything going on lately, he rarely had time to talk to Dumbway, or check on D-Day.

Huncho was in the kitchen, heating up noodles in the microwave when he heard Camry scream upstairs. He looked up and took off out the kitchen, grabbing his strap off the counter along the way. He rushed up the stairs, climbing them three at a time, and shot to their bedroom to find Camry holding the dresser, taking deep breaths, a wet spot beneath her on the floor.

"What!" What's goin—"

"My water broke!" she said, cutting him off. "Grab the keys!"

"Wha—How?" Huncho was incredulous. She wasn't due for at least another month and a half. "I thought—"

"Grab the fucking keys, Daldrick!" Camry placed her other hand over her stomach. "And wake Zakayla!"

Huncho took off to wake Zakayla and grab the keys. He dressed her quickly, phoned ahead to the hospital, and rushed back to the room to help Camry to the car as a light rain began to fall from the night sky. He secured Zakayla in the back seat, got in on the driver side and crunk the car up in a daze. He couldn't believe it. He was about to be a daddy again.

Backing out the driveway, he pulled off, heading to Tanner Medical Center, a hospital in Villa Rica.

***

Back in Atlanta at Grady Memorial Hospital, Marko stirred, eyes blinking open. He squinted from the sudden brightness of the light, looking around the room to find it empty.

He pushed the panic button, and within moments a team of nurses and doctors rushed in his room. Brandi and Meeka, who had just left moments before to go get something to eat, were coming down the hallway when they saw the hospital staff rushing into his room, and were immediately seized with panic. They rushed over to his room, but were stopped at the door by a white male nurse in powder blue scrubs.

"Hold on, give us a moment, you can't come in here."

"What's going on? Is he alright?" Brandi said. "Did he flatline? What—what happened?"

"I'm not exactly sure right now. We're responding to the panic button. It'll only take a few minutes to make sure he's stable, then we'll let you right in, okay?"

They nodded, and he went inside closing the door behind him, leaving them standing in the hallway in shock. Meeka was the first to speak.

"Oh, my god," she said. "Did he—He said—"

Brandi cut her off. "I'm calling Kay-Nay."

***

Heavy rain pelted the top of the stolen PT Cruiser, sitting out front of the Walmart in the crowded parking lot. Inside was Bam in the driver seat, Rock in the passenger seat, and in the back seat was Quamain, and Duckman. All of them were strapped.

After pulling up on Quamain earlier, they had decided tonight would be the night they put in some work. Outside of Woadie and Duckman, Quamain had been the first to embrace Southside Fam who wasn't from 1100 Block. Thus, two sets were established within Da Fam: 1100 Block Fam and 138 Fam. Bam was his first Famo, and for his first task: he was in charge of securing the whip for tonight's mission.

"A PT Cruiser?" Duckman had complained in disbelief upon initially seeing their getaway whip. "How the hell we gone look ridin' out on some Gangsta shit in a PT Cruiser?"

"Man, I don't know," Bam yelled. "Quamain told me to get a car, so I got a car. Goddamn!"

Bam was short, with a stocky build, and skin as black as a GD bandanna, with an attitude out this world. He always seemed mad, yet calm and would explode in a Usain minute.

Rock shrugged, getting in on the passenger side. "Where the hell you get this shit from anyways?"

Duckman and Quamain were climbing into the back seat, and Bam was suddenly chill. "Shiiid, I caught some old white bitch getting out her shit at the ATM in the Publix parking lot on 85." He crunk up the car. "Caught her old ass slippin'."

From Lake Ridge Parkway they swerved to Lovejoy, and rode through Tara Glynn, Greystone, and Panhandle, until they caught sight of Champ riding with TMC Skeet on Tara Road. Deciding to tail him, they followed him to a housing subdivision called The Meadows, where he dropped Skeet off, all the way to where they now sat in wait for him. He had been inside Walmart for a little over fifteen minutes now.

Duckman chuckled under his breath.

"W'sup?" Quamain said, eying a sexy group of females walking by under umbrellas.

"I still can't believe we 'bout to do this shit in a PT Cruiser."

Quamain laughed. "I know, right. But it's a good thing too, though. Ain't no nigga, bitch or cop expectin' nobody to pull a gutta move in a PT Cruiser. Look how long we just been followin' this nigga ass." Quamain paused to let it sink in. "We'd have tried that shit in a Crown Vic or a mufuckin Chevy, we woulda been gunnin' it out down Tara Boulevard on some hot shit."

"Speaking of hot shit," Rock pointed to a red and black Clayton County PD squad car slowly creeping by the front entrance sliding doors of Walmart. "We got company."

It reached the end of the building and circled around back, just as Champ was coming out holding three grocery bags in each hand. He paused, talking to a short brown-skinned cutie from the group that just walked by the car.

"Damn!" Duckman said. "What now?"

Rock, being the thinker he had always been, thought fast. This was Southside Fam's first move. He couldn't risk killing the momentum before it started. Besides, it wasn't just about the movement. This was about Thugga, and his defiance of Huncho's peace treaty. This wasn't a situation, this was his opportunity. His chance to set the tone for Da Fam, avenge his brother, say fuck Huncho, and gain the respect of the Mob all in one breath. Rock tied a brown bandanna around his face.

"Everybody relax. I got this. One shot." Rock cocked his .40. "Pull up on that nigga, Bam. When I buss his stupid ass, smash out."

"Shiiid, say no moe." Bam crunk the car, put the gear in reverse, backed out, put it in drive, and pulled around front.

The sound of the windshield wipers was the only thing to be heard as the PT Cruiser eased closer, but all Rock could hear was his own heartbeat drumming in his ears. The females were all smiles, and Champ was completely unsuspecting as they slowed to a stop behind him. His back was to them.

Rock pulled his black hoodie over his head and rolled down the window. "Yo Champ, remember me?"

Champ turned around and Rock stuck his pistol out the window.

Bwa!

A streak of blood shot from Champ's face as he staggered backward, bussing the back of his head on the pavement. Bam mashed his foot on the gas, burning out as the group of females that surrounded Champ began to scream, and the entire parking lot erupted in terror.

Rock yelled something out the window, as Bam shot up through the parking lot, fishtailing right onto Tara Boulevard, heading straight into Hampton. They were on their way to Griffin to lay low at Tony's.

The scene at Walmart was pure pandemonium. People were coming out of Walmart to the sight of Champ laid out cold, with a thick puddle of crimson red blood around his head that thinned out and ran down the cracks in the concrete as it mixed with the rain. Three squad cars had already responded to the incident, and police were already attempting to get ahold of the scene by pushing the screaming, hysterical girls back from his body and creating a perimeter. An ambulance could be heard closing in from a distance.

A black officer squatted beside Champ, placing two fingers on his neck. "He still has a pulse!"

The ambulance arrived and EMT personnel lifted him onto a stretcher as pedestrians stood by in the rain, watching on in shock. They loaded him into the back of the ambulance and peeled off.

At a McDonald's table inside Walmart, a skinny white uniformed officer was questioning the group of females Champ had been talking to when he was shot.

"And you're sure that's all the suspect said when the car pulled up?" he said, talking to the girl Champ had actually been talking to. "He asked the victim if he remembered him?"

"Um, they yelled something else out the window as they rode off."

The officer stood ready with his pen and pad. "Could you make out what it was that they said?"

She nodded, as the officer waited patiently. He could tell she was pretty shook up by the incident.

"It sounded like—like, he said—" She paused again unsure, using the end of her jacket sleeve to wipe her eyes.

"Yes?" the officer prodded on.

"Fam or suffer."

Elijah R. Freeman

Chapter 19

Huncho sat in the hospital waiting room of Tanner Medical Center, bouncing Zakayla on his lap. Camry had been in labor for eight hours, and he wanted so badly to be there with her to hold her hand, but there was no one to watch Zakayla, and the doctors had forbidden her to enter. So in the crowded waiting room it was, and to Huncho it felt like an eternity had gone by. He had phoned Mr. and Mrs. Watkins, and his mother, to let them know that their grandbaby had decided to come early, and had just not too long ago finally got ahold of Yummy, who promised she would be on her way to the hospital as soon as she got off work the following day.

Huncho was watching a video, which TD had sent, of Dreak performing at The Club House.

The Club House was a teen club on Tara Boulevard, and was the fourth establishment Dreak had performed at that week. His career had taken flight after opening for Gucci Mane and Waka Flocka Flame at a club called Primetime, on the eastside a week and a half after his first paid show at The Atrium. Huncho was proud of him. Most young niggas his age would have let the clout get to their head, got caught up, and played themselves off the street. Dreak was of a different breed of 90's babies, one who made the best decisions based off sound, unchanging principles. He could only imagine where he would be if he had the same mentality at his age. It took prison to snatch his life away and teach him that he couldn't talk his way out of problems he behaved himself into.

Zakayla tapped him on his shoulder. "Daddy, I'm hungry."

"Hungry?" Huncho put his phone away.

Zakayla nodded, wiping her eyes. "Uh-huh."

"What you want to eat, Kay-Kay?"

"Candy."

Huncho laughed. "You want some candy, baby?"

She nodded again.

Huncho chuckled, lifting her from his lap into his arms as he stood. "Come on, Little Foot. Let's go get you some candy."

He walked past the receptionist's desk to the vending machine, where Zakayla picked out a pack of Starburst. Sliding the quarters in the coin slot, he waited for them to drop, and reached into the bottom compartment to grab them. He bussed the pack open, tore the wrapper off a Starburst, and gave it to Zakayla who gladly put it in her mouth and began chewing. She smiled, and he kissed her on the cheek. A mother sitting with her son, who was apparently running a fever, was watching Huncho, smiling.

Huncho was headed back to his seat when a skinny white, red-haired female nurse in lavender scrubs and white flats came through the double doors that led to the back, holding a clip board.

"Daldrick Blanding."

Huncho paused, looking her way, thinking he'd rather she hadn't called his full name out like that. Considering how niggas these days were snitching! He gave the waiting room a once-over, and approached her.

"W'sup?"

"Blanding?"

"That's me."

The nurse smiled. "Follow me."

She turned around and walked back through the double doors, and Huncho followed close behind, holding Zakayla. They walked the length of the fairly empty hallway, and stopped in front of a huge glass window, through which they viewed a room full of babies asleep in incubators.

"There he is," she said, pointing to what seemed to Huncho like the smallest baby in the room. "Your new baby boy."

Huncho stared at the sleeping baby, amazed at the miracle of life. He had been in the county fighting a murder charge when Zakayla was born, so this was all new to him. He smiled, proud of the life he created.

"Look at ya lil brother, Kay-Kay," he said, pointing at the baby.

The nurse was all smiles, standing beside him. "Ms. Watkins is asleep from exhaustion. She did good. Have y'all decided on a name for him yet?"

The memory of Flame getting gunned down by the police flashed before his eyes, and his smile faded. He lowered his gaze, truly hurting inside for his homeboy and all that he never had the chance to experience. At the age of seventeen they swore they had the world figured out. You couldn't tell them they hadn't done it all. Looking back, he realized they didn't know shit. In all actuality, they hadn't even begun to live, and it set in that Flame would never know the joy of creating a life.

Noticing the change in his demeanor, the nurse lost her smile. "I'm sorry. Did I say something wrong?"

Huncho looked up, offering a weak smile. "Oh, naw. I'm just—I guess I'm just a lil overwhelmed emotionally, that's all."

Her smiled returned. "Oh, okay. That's understandable. So, you do have a name?"

Again, he thought of Flame.

"Yea," Huncho said. "Justin."

***

Marko was sitting up in bed in a white and blue paper gown, with an eye patch over his eye. Brandi and Meeka were standing on either side of him, and DJ Carleone was at the foot of his hospital bed. Kay-Nay and Frog were also present in the room. It was a foggy morning, and a misty drizzle was falling outside. Marko had just finished recounting his story to them, and they were at a loss for words, having never heard of a robbery occurring in the style in which he described quite similar to a Hollywood motion picture. To them, the whole story sounded like some movie shit. Nevertheless, it had happened. His injuries and the comatose state they had left him in was proof of that much.

According to what he could recall before he faded into unconsciousness, they were robbed by a gang of niggas dressed in police uniforms, and it turned out the niggas were actually Bloods.

"Oh, my god—Marko," Brandi said. "That's crazy. I'm so sorry you had to go through that."

"And you sure it wasn't the Mafia tryna throw you off?" DJ still wasn't convinced that Southside Mafia hadn't been involved.

"I'm positive," Marko said. "I ain't recognize nan one of 'em. These was some up top niggas. Besides, the cop uniforms was the throw off. Not the red bandannas."

Kay-Nay, who had been staring out the window at the foggy downtown Atlanta skyline, turned around, nodding. "I figured as much."

Everyone in the room turned their attention to him.

"What you mean?" Marko's expression was one of mass confusion.

"Me and Kebo was pullin' out of Old Town Villas when I got a call from Benzo. He was in the process of tellin' me to hit Brandi's line 'bout the lawyer she put on retainer, when I heard gunshots and a bunch of commotion in the background. Benzo must've dropped the phone or something, 'cause things got harder to hear in the background. All I caught was a nigga with a New York accent yell something about Blood Gang and demand some work." His gaze drifted to the floor, and he grew somber. "Kebo floored it, floating down Godby, but we didn't make it. By the time we pulled up, they were nowhere to be found, and someone had already called 12. We could hear sirens approaching from a distance."

This was the first time any of them had heard what Kay-Nay was telling them. He hadn't told Kebo all of what he heard, and they hadn't divulged the call to anyone.

DJ shrugged. "Fuck that shit. Know any Bloods?"

Frog shook his head. He was sitting on a chair up against the wall. "Not really. And even if we did, it's not that simple. It's all type of different Blood sets, and if you've been listenin' you might recall the fact that these niggas ain't from here."

Marko was in deep thought. Brandi and Meeka were staring at him.

DJ threw his arms up. "So what now?"

"We wait," Kay-Nay said, drawing the attention of the room back to him. "Their style ain't some shit they just came up with overnight. Whoever they are, they're seasoned, and just as sure as thirty-six zips make a brick, they'll strike again in a similar way. All we gotta do is follow the bread crumbs. That's when we pop."

Everybody in the room fell silent, but Kay-Nay was in his thoughts. He had a feeling that something big was about to jump off on the Southside. Like 2005 all over again, except this time, things would be much worse.

Chapter 20

Southside Fam was ten deep in the parking lot of the club house located in the center of Lake Ridge. The rising sun was beginning to clear up the fog, and they were three cars deep in wait for the Mob to pull up. Two days had passed since they caught Champ slippin' at the Walmart in Lovejoy, and the incident was the talk of Clayton County. It made both Channel 2 Action News and Fox 5, and had been more than enough for Dec, and any other Mob nigga for that matter. Today's link-up was to make the alliance official.

All ten Fam affiliates were posted around Rock's Cutlass, except for Bam and Bullethead, who were sitting inside listening to *Beat To Sleep,* the first Fam track. Sitting on the trunk was Quamain and his older brother Truth; standing around them, kicking shit, was TJ, Calvin, Duckman, Renda, and Noggin. Rock was leaned back against the driver side door, texting Kush, his female chop-shop connect from Hillandale in College Park.

The PT Cruiser was still in Tony's backyard under a tarp, and he needed her to have someone slide through with a tow truck to pick it up. Skinning Tony down daily was beginning to fuck with his funds. He hadn't been in the trap due to not fucking with the Mafia, and his mind had been too focused on other shit to hit a lick. Rock's phone vibrated, and he wasn't surprised to see that it was Tony texting for his daily duck off deposit. Shaking his head, he texted back that he would slide through later.

He looked up, and two cars – a silver Tesla and a dark blue Impala – were turning into the parking lot entrance. They pulled all the way down into the lot, one car parking beside them, the other parking across from them. Southside

Fam looked on as the cars cut their engines, and the doors opened.

Burnout got out the driver side of the Impala parked across from them. Dec got out on the passenger side, and Rio and Hot-Deezy got out the back. Bam and Bullethead got out of Rock's car and posted up against the ride. Hopping out the Tesla parked to their right two spaces down were four Mobsters Rock knew as Amp, Parkway Red, Ammo, and Bizzy, all of whom were rocking orange bandannas.

Burnout walked up to Rock and dapped him up. "Whaddup, boi?"

"W'sup, foo?" Rock looked behind him at Dec. "That good enough for you?"

Dec was nodding with a smirk, rocking a shirt on which *Free Bama & E-Meezy* was monogrammed. Beneath the shirt, he wore blue jeans with a whitish tint. "I ain't gone flex, you went ham. I'm fuckin' wit'cha."

He embraced Rock in a handshake hug, as the rest of Da Fam joined the huddle.

"So what, we cliqued up?" Duckman said. "Fuck we callin' this shit?"

Bam shrugged. "23 Fam Mob?"

Bullethead sucked his teeth. "Fuck naw! That shit sound lame as fuck."

Bam's jaw muscles twitched as he mugged Bullethead, mumbling "Fuck that shit" under his breath.

"How 'bout Mob Family?" Ammo said. "Forget the 23. They'll know w'sup with us. Southside Family, Murk Mob, M.O.B 23 and Parkway. Mob Family. Far as our colors, we continue to rock our own individual colors. Brown and orange."

Everyone standing around was nodding.

"So everybody in agreement with *Mob Family*?" Burnout said, looking around.

"Hell yea."

"Yea, that's straight."

"Cool with me."

Seeing that they were all in agreement, Burnout shrugged. "*Mob Family* it is." He stuck his hand out. "Always us."

Rock shook it. "Never them."

***

In Lovejoy, JT and Mickey came to a screeching halt, curbside, out front a cobblestone house that served as a Trigga Mafia trap headquarters. Gino, Dru, Skeet and a few other TMC affiliates, were on the porch smoking, chillin' and waiting for plays to pull up when they hopped out.

"Fuck y'all niggas got goin' on!" Mickey was furious as he walked into the front yard, JT right behind him. "Y'all ain't heard? My mufuckin' brother died on the way to the hospital with a hole in his mouth!"

"Who?" Skeet said.

"Champ, nigga! Ron been in juvenile two weeks now."

Dru was snubbing out a blunt, a look of disbelief etched on his face. "Whoa, wait a minute. I knew Ron got knocked for an AR, but when the fuck—"

"Man y'all pussy ass niggas know what's goin' on," JT jumped in, cutting him off. "This shit all over MySpace and the news. This shit like Lil Richie all over again. Niggas poppin' us and ain't nan nigga stressin' TMC shook shit."

Dru's expression switched to anger, as he jumped to his feet. "Hold up, bra, who the fuck you callin' a pussy-ass nigga? Y'all poppin' that big boy shit to us, nigga yeen bussed shit neither, nigga!"

"Fuck you tawmbout!" Skeet co-signed.

Gino nodded.

"Man, fuck y'all niggas." Mickey shot a bird at the porch. "I'll never throw up another 'M' again in my muthafuckin life. Let's ride, JT."

"I don't give a fuck!" Dru yelled at their backs as they walked off. "If you wanna get technical, ain't nan one of you niggas killed shit!"

The TMC affiliates co-signed behind him.

"You must forgot, Mickey," Skeet said. "We took Thugga out with Ron 'bout what happened to Nard. Me, Dee-Dee, and Gino. Now, show me where yo rank at! All that hollerin'. Nigga, get some straightenin'!"

Mickey was nodding with his eyes narrowed, as he opened the driver side door of his black Honda Civic and climbed in. JT got in on the passenger side.

Mickey crunk up the car. "They think this shit a game."

"Don't e'en trip," JT said. "I got a lil cousin named Wooh, stay out in Jurrasic Park. He a part of some new B-B-A 9-Tre Blood Gang movement. They got smoke with the Mafia, and we got Intel that could get us in good with the set."

Mickey pulled off from the curb. "So where to?"

"Hickory Park."

***

Agent Smith was back in Virginia after losing Purp to the streets and failing to collect a witness, or solid evidence that could link Huncho to the Espinoza investigation. However, if he could not win, he was determined not to lose. Refusing to be an assed out field agent, he had proceeded with the indictment against Ricardo Espinoza. Now, no one could call him a failure. He had done his part by building the case against him. It was on the attorney general's office to convict him.

He reached the Marine Corps Base, Quantico, one of the largest U.S. Marine bases in the world, and also home to a basketful of federal law enforcement platforms. The facility was behind high fences with a guard gate where serious men in uniform stood holding automatic weapons.

Smith drove his gray Dodge Durango up to the gate, rolled down his window, and drew a long breath, thinking about the mysterious death of his former partner Whitfield, and his subsequent finding in an abandoned warehouse with his slaughtered family. He punched his access code in, flashed his credentials, and pulled through the base entrance, wondering for the millionth time if Whitfield's unfortunate end had anything to do with the Espinoza case. Carlos had already been discovered conspiring to put hits on the Mexican DEA agents and several other entities involved with their case that had set them up. Having failed, he saw no other way out than to turn State's witness. But what if Ricardo had succeeded where Carlos failed?

It was already suspected that he had his brother's family executed, which was highly plausible. He wasn't sure how exactly, but it was definitely a possibility. Without proof, though, he was pulling straws.

He pulled in front of a brick building, which also housed, among other things, the FBI Academy, lab, and ViCAP – Violent Criminal Apprehension Program. He climbed out the car, buttoned his jacket, and made his way inside, headed to speak with Special Agent Boykins – head of ViCAP. He'd received an email from him requesting to meet at the ViCAP

131

building at 9 a.m. sharp in regard to an ongoing investigation, which initially struck him as odd, considering the fact that he had never worked that field or interacted with that particular agent before. Formed in 1985, ViCAP was the unit dealing with serial murders, and other violent crimes usually of the sexual nature. They were part of the Critical Incident Response Group (CIRG).

Smith reached the door, opened it, and walked inside.

***

Watching him enter from across the street, in a tan pick-up truck, was Dinero, who had disguised himself in a fake wig, a deceptive Chuck Norris-looking mustache, dark shades, a navy blue jumpsuit with the nametag *Pedro* on it, and a pair of tall black water boots. From the pick-up truck, he'd been watching the ViCAP entrance from the McDonald's parking lot. Having his photo taken and forged onto the FBI credentials he had stolen off Whitfield, he was able to use it to gain entry to the base. He grabbed a tool box off the front seat, checked his reflection once more in the sun visor mirror, and hopped out the truck on a mission. He slammed the door, and speed walked to the corner, looking both ways before crossing the street.

***

The first thing Smith noticed when he walked in through the ViCAP entrance was that the place was fairly empty, void of any major activity.

Maybe that's why he chose this day to meet, he thought.

Up ahead an Asian female agent was locking up the lab. She finished, and turned to leave, walking in his direction.

"Excuse me," he said, addressing her. "Um, do you know where I can find Special Agent Boykins? I have a meeting with him today at 9 a.m."

A confused expression crossed her face. "That's strange."

"How so?" Smith said, feeling as though he had missed something.

"Well," she shook her head. "He hasn't been here all morning. In fact, he won't be here at all. He's out for the day, meeting with the National Center for the Analysis of Violent Crime."

It was Smith's turn to look confused. "You—are you sure?"

"Positive. You didn't get the memo?"

Smith sighed. "Apparently not, I guess."

She shook her head, smiling. "Don't sweat it. May have been an honest mistake."

"Yea," Smith said. "You're probably right. Typo on the date or something. I'll just email him to reconfirm."

"Okay, sure thing." She walked off, and Smith watched after her, taking a moment to admire her curvy frame.

I need to get laid, he thought as he headed back to his car, cursing Boykins mentally for wasting his time, though he honestly had nothing better to do. He had yet to be reassigned to another case.

He exited the building just in time to see the Asian agent get into the driver side of a baby blue Nissan Murano, just four parking spaces down from his car. There were only three other cars in the parking lot. A line of tan military Hum Vee's rode by. As he unlocked his door, a pick-up truck with a Hispanic driver pulled out of a McDonald's parking lot across the street, turning right in line behind them.

He got in his car and crunk it up. The engine stalled, but didn't start.

Smith looked at the dash. "What the—"

He tried it again. Just then the entire car exploded, erupting in flames, sending a billowing mushroom cloud sky-high. The Asian woman screamed, looking on in fear as bystanders rushed forward to see what they could do to help, but it was all in vain. Smith was long gone.

Chapter 21

Huncho was on the expressway, headed to Riverdale, to drop Zakayla off with his mother for the weekend so he could handle some Break-Free Records business. He had left the hospital after Yummy arrived with Jay to keep Camry company. He signed the birth certificate, and was out of there. They were in the process of finalizing Dreak's mixtape, whose title had been changed from '*I'm Really From Dat South*' to '*Triggadale*.' He got off the expressway, turning left onto Old Dixie. His phone rang, as he pulled to a stop at the light on Tara Boulevard and Upper Riverdale Road.

"Yo!" Huncho answered his phone, to which no one responded. "Hello?"

"We need to speak," a voice said.

"We speakin'. Who this?"

"Ricardo."

Huncho paused, skeptical. The light turned green, and he put his foot on the gas, crossing the four-way onto Upper Riverdale. "Ricardo who?"

"Espinoza."

"The first time I brought Cam out west, what strip did you meet me on? Three seconds or I'm hanging up."

"Really?"

"Yea, really," Huncho said. "Two seconds."

"Rodeo Drive. Too easy."

"Haaa, what's up, my bwoy! "Huncho laughed. "Man, no other shit. You don't know how happy I am to hear from you, right now."

Ricardo laughed. "Is that so?"

"Hell yea! It's a mean ass drought on solid niggas in the game out here. You don't know the half."

"Believe me. I have an idea." Ricardo chuckled. "It's part of the reason I'm making this call."

"What's the word?"

"Well for starters, word is that you're to blame for the murder of Purp." Huncho was about to cut in, but Ricardo stopped him short. "Ah-Ah-Ah, I know. You had nothing to do with it."

"Y-you do?"

"Of course," Ricardo said. "I also know who was behind it and why."

"Who?"

"A Blood by the name of O.G Billy Trello. He was commissioned by Billiano to acquire turf for a sub-chapter of the cartel ran by two distant cousins of mine named, Diego and Placido, operating out of New York."

"Trello." Huncho's brain drew a blank as he passed by Southern Regional, wishing Justin had been born there instead of some hospital in the boonies. He snapped back to the conversation at hand. "I don't think I know no Trello, bra."

"I know you don't, but Huncho, listen to me. There's something you need to know."

"What?"

"There's a bounty on your head. The Blood Gang has officially declared war on 2-DUB Mafia."

"Bloods? A fuckin' gang! For what?"

"For territory." Ricardo said. "Listen to me, Huncho. 2-DUB Mafia runs the Southside, and they want in."

"So what the fuck! I'm 'posed to lay down 'cause they work for your people?"

"If so, would we be on the phone having this conversation?" Huncho was silent. Ricardo went on. "I am not telling you to do any such thing. On the contrary, I wish you the best. Not just that but I intend to help you. You are loyal. Dependable. I like the way you move. So, this is a warning."

Click!

The line went dead.

***

"Chow call! Chow call!" Old Skool yelled.

The dorm entrance door clicked furiously, sounding like rapid fire as Ms. Mackey, an older brown-skinned female officer, pressed the button repeatedly to get the dorm's attention.

Glancing at the booth to find Ms. Mackey doing a scooping-fork gesture, inmates headed to their rooms to prepare to fall out to eat.

Hearing the commotion, Dumbway got up from his bunk, phone pressed to his ear as he conversed with his girl, Shatoya. He cracked his door, and saw that the dorm was gathering at the booth waiting to file out through the sally-port.

"Aye—say, bae," he said, cutting off her rundown of the proper way to go about acquiring pure bread pits. "Let me catch this chow call movement. I gotta catch this play in the kitchen. I 'ma hit ya soon as I get back, a'ight?"

"Okay, baby."

"Okay. Love you."

"I love you, too." She said. "Oh, Demarcus!"

Dumbway paused, finger on the red call button. "What's up?"

"Don't forget, okay. Call me as soon as you get back. I wanna finish telling you while it's still fresh on my mind."

A smile teased the corner of his mouth. He sucked his teeth, knowing her true motive. "You know you just wanna talk to a nigga."

"So!" She was smiling, and he could tell. "I want to talk to you. Call me right back, okay? I'm serious. My phone's on the charger. I can't keep it on me and I don't wanna miss your call. Last time, you got side tracked shooting dice and left me hanging."

"I got yooou!" They both laughed. "Naw bae, dead ass. I'm there and back. Wait by the phone, a'ight?"

She said *alright,* and they hung up just as the dorm entrance door popped, and the inmates began filing out into the sally-port.

Rushing, Dumbway got state-dressed, and snatched three packs of tobacco from his stash. He dropped his phone in, and stood, sucking in his stomach to stuff the packs in his boxer briefs. He reached in his locker box to grab his belt, but stopped abruptly, double-taking at his door window. He could've sworn he saw someone peeking in. Dismissing it, he grabbed his belt, figuring someone stopped by to see if he heard the door click. Nothing unusual. Common, even. In fact, the last four years behind the wall had taught him the gesture was actually a good thing. Another sign that the dorm was chain-gang.

"Last call for chow!"

"Shit!" Dumbway hurried out the room, fixing his belt as he sprinted down the stairs. Miss the last call on Ms. Mackey's shift, and he was dead in a Chevy. He hated when she worked. He glanced in the booth, slipping out the door just before it slammed shut.

The obvious look of disappointment etched on her face stopped him dead in his tracks. His face twisted in contempt. "Goddamn!"

Mean-mugging, she jammed her finger in the direction of the chow hall. "Go!"

Dumbway shook his head and walked off to avoid getting locked down on a humbug. It was crazy to him how it seemed like the black C.O's were worse than the white ones.

Damn, that hoe need some dick, he thought.

The sky was a cold baby blue, with no trace of clouds in sight. Overhead, a small two-seater airplane flew by, and Dumbway looked up, wishing he was in it.

He jogged across the small yard to catch up with the rest of the dorm at the gate, as they crossed the walk into the chute. Everyone in, the officer locked the chute, and they made their way around the bend to the chow-hall.

"Man, this chute shit some bull," Showtime said. He walked a few steps ahead of Dumbway, alongside Stutterbox Ced. "In the Feds—"

"M-m-maaan, shut yo b-bitch ass up!" Stutterbox Ced cut in. "Tired of you runnin' yo m-m-muuu, mufuckin' mouth. 'Bout the—godammit! 'B-bout the Feds! Shiiid, nobody tryna hear that shhh-shi—that shit!"

Everyone laughed.

Showtime was visibly embarrassed. "Shiiid, don't nobody wanna—"

"Hear me stu-stutter?" Ced said, cutting him off. "I know. So what nigga, f-fuck ya!"

Dumbway smiled as once again, everybody laughed. Robbed of his only comeback, Showtime waved him off in frustration, but let it go.

"Bout time," someone mumbled behind him.

Dumbway looked back and locked eyes with a white boy, who – by the apologetic look in his eyes – had apparently made the comment. Probably thinking he and Showtime were cool. There was a shorter white boy beside him, looking equally as scared, but Dumbway was as tired of hearing Showtime comparing everything that happened in the State to the Feds as the next man.

"Yooo, Red Rag!" The voice came from a window as they passed G-building, drawing Dumbway's attention to the three Bloods straggling in the rear.

"What's up, twin?" the mid-height, brown-skinned, nappy temp rocking guy, who was obviously Red Rag, said.

"You got that 0-1-9?"

"Yea, I got it, Five."

"Now!"

Red Rag cut his eyes at Dumbway, and he turned away, realizing he was in his mouth. He pushed on, minding his business until the line came to a stop at the gate just ahead. Posting back at a distance behind the dorm, he scanned the faces exiting the chow hall, trying to figure out what dorm it was, until he caught sight of a familiar face he could've sworn he knew on the streets.

I know that ain't Brando flexin' ass, he thought. Just as he was about to call out to him, he felt someone coming up behind him.

"Blatt!"

Dumbway turned, and caught the gleam of sun on steel, before feeling a piercing sting in his cheek.

"Aargh!" He weaved, attempted to duck and roll on reflex, only to catch a blade to the back of his head, sending blood streaming down his neck.

Before he knew what was going on, he was getting poured out.

"Blood Gang!" one yelled, punching him.

Dumbway rushed him to the fence, head butting him, leaving blood on his forehead. Drawing his head back to go in, he kicked himself on the inside.

It was Red Rag who had just stabbed him. A call had been made on his life, but for what?

No time to be surprised, he went in for another head butt, only to be snatched backwards by his collar to the ground, drawing attention when the fence rattled. Inmates in and outside the chute looked on as he was stabbed relentlessly. Everyone inside stepped back, wanting nothing to do with the incident.

"Code One!" a skinny white brunette Corrections Officer yelled into the radio, catching sight of the ambush from the other side of the compound. "I repeat Code One in front of the chow hall!"

Corrections Officers rushed to respond to the call from all over the compound, but they were too far.

He was done for.

Too weak from blood loss to fight back, Dumbway went limp. Crimson red blood painted the ground inside the chute and dripped from the fabric of his state clothes. His last thought was of Shatoya waiting for him by her phone.

Then his world went black.

Chapter 22

It was the middle of the day. Huncho, TD, and Dreak were in a neon green tinted studio room at Visions Studios, out in Chamblee. The room was a 15-by-27 foot space, not including the inside of the booth behind the large sound-proof glass, in front of which was a waist-high platform with state-of-the-art equalizers on top. Having already completed his *Triggadale* mixtape prior to their visit, Dreak wasn't in the booth, but seated beside Jet, giving his input on the mixing down of his tracks. Huncho and TD were sitting on the V-shaped sectional in the corner, TD texting, Huncho in deep thought about the Intel he had just received from Ricardo about the Blood Gang bounty on his head, and the ensuing war that was soon to come.

It seemed crazy to him that just as he was preparing to make his departure from the game, he was being faced with his greatest challenge yet. He had come to the studio prepared to have a talk with TD about leaving Rock in charge in his place, as he moved on with his life's next venture, whatever it may be. The only thing he wanted part of was Break-Free Records, which he would help manage from a distance until he successfully established other businesses elsewhere.

With the Blood Gang threat at hand, he needed to call a meeting to make sure everyone was on point, and see if anyone had heard of a Blood named Trello. He believed in shooting first, and after the way Nard had crept him with Trigga Mafia, he refused to sit back and disregard a potential enemy, let alone one he had received word on, from a reliable source, that they had declared war on him. He had done a lot of growing up since his high school days, but the streets had him fucked up. It wasn't nothing to buss his guns, or have some shots fired. Every Mafioso throwing up an "M" was down to slide. He just wanted to have a word with a few choice affiliates about everything that was going on, and establish them as his new inner circle, one that would govern the affairs of the entire 2-DUB Mafia. They would be *The Elect*.

The only thing holding him up: Rock had changed his number, and nobody in the Mafia knew where he was.

He saw on the news a little over a week ago that Champ had been shot in front of the Walmart in Lovejoy. He survived at the scene, only to die on the way to Grady Memorial Hospital because Southern Regional didn't have a trauma center. There was no doubt in his mind that Champ's murder would inevitably fall back on him, but he had a good mind to believe that somehow, someway, Rock was behind it. He smelled treachery.

His phone rang and he answered on the second ring. "Whats up, Bra?"

"They killed my brother, man!" It was Longway, and he didn't sound good at all. "Some Blood niggas killed Dumbway, man. He dead. What the fuck!"

Huncho dropped the phone.

***

"And this a whole thang?" Rock said.

He, Duckman, Quamain and Bullethead, had come with Pint—a frontline M.O.B 23 Hard official—to Campbellton Road in Atlanta, to shop with Pint's cousin, Splurge – who had a spot in Shamrock Gardens. They were in the small dining room of one of the apartments, and Splurge had just sat a brick on top of the faux-wood dining table.

"Fuckin' right," he said in response to Rock. "We can drop it on the scale if you want."

"Let's do that," Rock said. "You got some Arm & Hammer in this bitch?"

Splurge nodded. "Yea, why?"

"Cause I'ma wanna drop a duce if the weight checks out. You cool with that?"

Splurge glanced at Pint, who nodded. "Shiiid, yea, you good. Let me go grab this shit, real quick."

Splurge walked off down the hallway to a back room.

Rock turned to Pint. "What was the glance all about?"

"Man, cuz, just shell, bra. That's all," Pint said. "Been doin' this shit since I was in elementary. He done seen too much. He just wanted to know if you were good, I guess. Wit' you tryna drop a duce in his kitchen and all."

"Any nigga buyin' a quarter bird or better should."

Pint shook his head. "Not his clientele. He only serves a handful throughout the city. That's how he's lasted this long. Stayin' true to a chosen few."

"Please," Duckman said. "Ain't that much trust in the world."

"Hell naw," Quamain agreed.

Pint shrugged it off, neglecting to respond.

"Aye, can we smoke in here?" Bullethead said. "I'm nickin' like a mufu—"

He cut it short as Splurge came walking back out carrying a triple beam scale and a glass pot, inside of which was a glass beaker. Sitting it on the table, he went to work, weighing everything up for them to see with their own eyes: thirty-six ounces. Rock scooped two random ounces from the brick, and stepped in the kitchen to do what he did best.

Pint was right behind him. "You sure you know what you doin'?"

Rock shot him a look. "Who you think cooked up most of the rocks 2DM was pushin'?"

Brows raised, Pint shrugged. "Say no more."

Duckman came in the kitchen and hopped up on the counter, to sit and watch. He looked to Splurge. "You don't mind, do you?"

"Naw, you good." Splurge turned to Rock. "The baking soda's in the fridge."

Bullethead and Quamain took a seat in two of the four chairs around the dining room table, as Rock made his way to the fridge. Opening it, he smiled, shaking his head. Wasn't shit in there but an empty egg carton, a generic juice jug filled with water, a block of government cheese in the side compartment and in the back, an open box of baking soda. He grabbed it.

We most definitely in the trap, he thought.

Fifteen minutes later: Rock was holding up a Pyrex, watching the twirling water rock up.

He smiled. "Yo Q, go grab the bread from the trunk. We in there."

"In the trunk?"

Rock sucked his teeth, shaking his head vigorously. "Naw, fool. The—man, go get the money, bra."

After paying Splurge and exchanging numbers, they packed up the brick, hopped in Rock's 1972 Cutlass Supreme heading back to 1100 Block. Pint was in his own whip, headed to Bonanza.

Rock thought long and hard about what his next move would be. He had rode on Trigga Mafia in Thugga's name. Now he just wanted the paper, but wasn't sure what the repercussions of his actions would be. One thing he was keenly aware of was that while we as humans were endowed with free will of choice, we had no control over the consequences that came as a result of those choices. Whenever someone picked up one side of a stick, they inadvertently picked up the other side as well. Good or bad, for Thugga, he didn't give a fuck. It is what it is, 'cause it was what it was.

They would probably blame 2-DUB Mafia anyways, which brought him to the next checkpoint station of his train of thought. When they did, where would that leave him and Huncho?

Personally, he had no animosity towards Huncho, and didn't intend to spark a beef with 2-DUB Mafia. All the way real, he had no intentions on starting a turf war over lucrative trap spots either, which would be a major blow to them, considering he knew their operation inside-out. No, he had used the last of what he saved to cop a brick, and with it he would flood the unclaimed territory or traps run by those of whom he had no previous ties. He had a game plan in mind to make the Mob Family one of the Southside's elite organizations, and planned to see it through to its entirety. But technically, hadn't he done just that when he cliqued up with the M.O.B., who were their sworn enemies?

As far as a legitimate hustle, he hadn't decided on anything concrete as of yet, but he was thinking. He didn't want to do the music industry thing, but he would stand behind Murk Mob, who had mentioned an interest in the industry. He himself would seek success elsewhere.

Elijah R. Freeman

Chapter 23

Razor had just been a part of a three-man team of Billy's that had been chosen by Hitman to jump in two new homies, one of whom was Wooh's cousin; a heavy dark-skinned guy named JT, who had a circle face and thick wavy hair. The other was a short, dirty, brown-skinned young nigga named Mickey: he had unforgiving eyes, and rocked his hair in two big puff balls, one to the left, the other to the right.

Both had seemed familiar to Razor when they showed up at the headquarters in Hickory Park the previous day, and his suspicions had been confirmed when they brought the Trigga Mafia trap in Greystone to Hitman's attention. They were TMC, and had been on the scene at the car wash the day Thugga and Woadie murked Pit. He had seen them on the news as they stood with Mel later that day. He wasn't worried about them, though. They had never crossed paths during his time as a Mafioso, and he doubted they knew of his treachery, or the fact that he had run to the police after it blew up in his face. All the same, their initiation being so close to home made him conscious of the fact that someone who did know he was a rat coming home was highly unlikely, but possible. All it took was a disagreeable circumstance, and like JT, Mickey and himself, a former comrade was subject to go renegade all to conspire against the clique they had once pledged their loyalty to.

As for his plans to use the Blood Gang to take out Huncho and contribute to the collapse of 2-DUB Mafia, everything was right on schedule. A list of trap spots to hit had been made, and he had personally made sure The Spot was on there. Huncho was a marked man and a walking lick. The entire B-B-A 9-Tre Blood set was looking for him, and though no one had seen him, let alone caught up with him since Trello had declared war on him a week ago, it was only a matter of time.

***

Billiano hung up the phone, having completed his conversation with Trello. Good news: Two new homies, who had inside Intel on a major trap spot run by their former clique in the Clayton County area, had been brought home the other day. They planned to hit it early next week, which was great news actually because, according to them, no other organization in that city posed a threat to their takeover of turf. He could hardly wait to call Placido with the news.

Billiano was a heavy five foot nine, with a big head that sat atop his stocky shoulders. His skin was the color of dark, rich soil, and was covered with tattoos, gang tattoos mostly, that he had got while serving a bid upstate. Some of which were in his face.

Born and raised in Harlem, New York, he was the epitome of a street savage. At the age of fifteen he was already a young Don, a wild one. Chain-gang had taught him structure, and he used it to organize his hood. He started his own Blood set on Rikers Island, and worked his way up within the ranks. By the time he got out, his set B-B-A 9-Tre was heavy at war with another East coast Bloodset, Sex-Money-Murder. And though he hadn't exactly won the war, the work he had put in had earned him respect in all five boroughs in the city of New York. His name was one to be feared, and not just because of the countless lives he had taken, but also because he was still standing. He wasn't dead or in jail like many of the Big Homies of his time. Billy had spread down the East coast, and infiltrated the rap industry, catching the attention of a few cartel members looking for certified street gangs who they could count on to move vast quantities of drugs. The rest was history.

Three years following their first front, they had flourished and had some success. All seemed well until his younger brother, Certified, had been murdered a year ago. He was in Virginia at the time carrying out the same mission Trello was heading now, a territory exposition. Back then, Trello was the High for Certified's line. Billiano would secure the work from Placido in New York, and Trello was the road runner. He would pick up the work and bring it back to Certified, from whose hand it would be distributed to different Billy Blood Gang affiliates in established territories they had claimed throughout their conquest and set up shop. It was while he was away during one of these various trips that Certified was murdered. Billiano had been devastated.

With Trello having been in charge of the pick-up and distribution, not to mention the fact that he had been second in command to Certified, Billiano gave him his own line and made him the Godfather. A year had passed. Nothing had come up short, and he had done nothing but make progress. Life was good, but the search for his brother's killer was still on, though the trail had long since run cold.

Chapter 24

Tamara Miller awoke at the sound of her house phone ringing atop her night stand. Shifting under the covers, she took a peek at the digital clock, which glowed a green 6:12 beside the ringing V-Tech phone. Sucking her teeth, she snatched the phone from the receiver in frustration, wondering who on Earth could possibly be calling her this early in the morning. She answered on the fifth ring, ready to go off.

"Hello?"

There was a pause, in which no voice could be heard on the other end, but what sounded like a busy city.

She glanced at the Caller ID, and put the phone back to her face, not recognizing the number. "Hello?"

"Ma—"

"W-who is—" she began, but stopped. She only had one child. "Antonio?"

There was another pause. "Come get me."

"Come get you?" Tamara was confused. To her knowledge, her son was hours away in another state. "From where?"

"Downtown Atlanta." His reply was punctuated by the blaring horn of a passing eighteen-wheeler. "I just got off the Greyhound. I uuuh—Can you just please come pick me up? I'll tell you everything when you get here. Just—please."

Tamara sighed. "Let me get dressed."

"You're—you're on your way?" he asked, sounding somewhere between surprised and elated.

She sat up in bed, back against the headboard. "Yes, Antonio, once I'm dressed, I'll be there."

Antonio was quiet for a moment, before speaking again. "I know what you thinkin' but don't worry. I got you, okay?"

Tamara, lost in her thoughts, was staring blankly at her window curtain, observing the orange glow from the street lights illuminating the other half of her room. They were still on, which meant the sun had yet to rise.

"I love you, ma," Antonio said, unable to think of anything else to say, yet feeling a need to fill in a silence his conscious told him he deserved.

She shook her head, bemused. "I love you, too."

Tamara hung up, and arose from the bed, heading to the bathroom to brush her teeth and wash her face. Hitting the light on, she grabbed her toothbrush and toothpaste, beginning as she contemplated the drastic change in her son since he started middle school. He had gone from an A and B honor roll student to a regular in the principal's office. The fighting. Weed smoking. Constant calls from his teachers to inform her of his constant disrespect, and numerous unexplainable absences. It was as if her son had been swapped out with a delinquent from that *Scared Straight* show she watched from time to time. The school riot at the end of his 9th grade year had been the last straw, after he ended up in the back of a Clayton County Police squad car. She withdrew him the following day, and sent him to Akron, Ohio, to live with his Aunt.

He begged and begged to come back all summer, but she was adamant in her refusal to let him return. Somehow, though, he was back. She would figure out how, when she got downtown, but she had already decided to let him stay. Fully dressed, she grabbed her keys and headed outside to her car, hoping she could trust him, and that she wasn't making a mistake.

***

It was a cold day with gray skies, and 2-DUB Mafia was swamp deep in Longway's backyard in Bridlewood, among them Southside and 220 Queens. The trees were bare, and on the ground the leaves had fallen, much like their respected comrade: Dumbway.

The mood was somber.

No one spoke as Huncho, who had just received word of Dumbway's murder the night before, entered the backyard, walking through the entrance of the tall wooden fence, flanked by TD, Slap-Rocks and Tall-Tezzee. The crunching of the yellowish-orange leaves announced his presence, and the crowd parted to make way for him. He passed Jayvo, who was biting his lip as tears fell from his eyes. Beside him, another Mafioso named Poohdalini was staring at the ground in a daze.

Huncho pushed on to the center where Longway stood black and tall, his neck-length dreads hanging free, except for the front that he had rubber-banded to stick up. Today wasn't the day to hide behind his locs. His big bra was gone and though he shed no tears, he wanted the world to see the pain in his eyes. He wore black and white low top Air Force Ones, baggy Coogi pants that he wore with a slight sag, and an all-black *"R.I.P Dumbway"* T-shirt with an old picture of Dumbway throwing up the M's. It had been cropped out of the first deep Southside Mafia photo taken. They were in front of the Riverdale High School gym in the bus lane on a hot summer weekend, on their way to Shoota's house in Roundtree Forest. Huncho was the youngest and smallest of the bunch, and had just got down the day before. He was holding a black 9mm, throwing up the "M's" between D-Day and B-Smeezee. TD and Ski had also been in the picture, along with Fred and Kasaan, who were still in chain-gang.

Huncho embraced Longway in a handshake hug. "Yeen e'en gotta say it, bra. It's on you. Don't worry. We finna go slaughter-gang on these pussy ass niggas. Real talk." He pulled back, giving Longway a reassuring tap on the shoulder.

Longway nodded.

Huncho turned to address the Mafia at last. "Since 2003 the Mafia's been holdin' shit down for the Southside. We put the south on the map. Before us, before 2-DUB, Riverdale was just another underrated city in the metro Atlanta area. But we put on and we still here. Through all the wars. The droughts. The indictments. The betrayal. The hatin'. Still we stand! And now what?" He paused, looking into the eyes of the many faces in the crowd. "We got some Blood niggas from North Bubbafuck call themselves declaring war on us to take what we've built. What we shed blood for. What we lost lives for. Then they kill one of our heads. One of the very Mafiosos who helped put this shit together."

He swept his gaze back over the crowd. "You let a mufucka slide and before long niggas is ice skatin'. Fuck that! We bussin' off the rip on anything bangin' red!"

"Hold up, I got family that's Blo—" a Mafioso named Silencer started, but stopped short when Huncho drew down on him.

"Mafia or nothin'?" Huncho said.

Silencer was taken back. "Huncho, bra, you—"

"Mafia or nothin'!" Huncho yelled, putting the pistol point blank range to the center of his forehead.

"You know I'm—"

Bwa!

Silencer's brains flew out the back of his head, and the crowd recoiled as his body crumpled to the ground.

Huncho pointed at his body. "Let this be a message to anybody who think he fuckin' with us halfway. We must only pledge allegiance to those who will fight with us and for us. Mafia or nothin'. Dub or die. If they ain't with us, they against us!"

Everyone stared at Silencer whose body laid akimbo, eyes staring into eternity, a bloody red dot in the middle of his forehead.

Huncho turned to Longway. "Meet me at The Spot in an hour. Come alone."

Just like that, he was back.

***

Up the street, Tone rode by the Bridlewood neighborhood sign, cruising down Taylor Road in his mother's gray Taurus. They had stopped at the McDonald's on 85 on the way home after she picked him up from the Greyhound bus station. As he ate his Big Mac, he thought on how he had saved up his money shoveling snow out of people's driveways for the past month, for a Greyhound ticket, then ran away in the middle of the night. Well, that's what he told his mother. His aunt, Buck, had bought the ticket for him. She was down with the whole thing. He loved his auntie, but her nigga was some bullshit, and they stayed bumping heads about one thing or another. If it wasn't the television, it was the time he came in. If it wasn't the time he would come in, it was where he had been. If it wasn't about where he had been, it was who he was hanging with, which irked him because he didn't even know that nigga. He was only family because he married his aunt.

Tone shrugged it off. He was back in his city. Riverdale, Georgia. Where he was born and raised. And though it was winter here, also, it seldom snowed if it did at all.

"Remember your promise, now, Antonio," his mother said. "No trouble."

"I got you, ma."

She eased on the brakes as they approached Brooks Crossing Apartments, and made a left, turning in. They pulled up in front of their building, across from which was a playground. Sitting on the bench, posted with a group of kids around his age, were his two closest friends, Monte and Booman. Tone and his mother got out, and she made her way inside, while Tone opened the backdoor to grab his suitcase off the backseat. Monte and Booman were walking up as he closed the door.

"So, your plan worked, I see," Monte said, dapping him up. He was dark-skinned like Tone and stood three inches above Tone's six-foot-one frame. His hair was low, unkempt, and he was seventeen – two years older than Tone and Booman.

Tone had put Monte and Booman on game about his plan, telling them that if he didn't come back home today, he had failed.

"You already slo." Tone dapped Booman up. "My nigga, B-O-O to the mufuckin' Meezy."

"Wassup, boi." Booman stepped back, nodding with a smile. "Back, I see."

"Hell yea."

Booman and Tone were the same height, but Booman's skin was black as a starless night, and his shoulder-length dreads were dyed brown halfway down. He was draped in all black, and Tone couldn't help but notice the gray bandanna tied through his belt loop in the front.

"Called Lauren yet?" Booman said, making Monte smile.

"Naw, not yet." Tone didn't care. Lauren was his boo. He planned to call her soon as he went in the house. "What? I don't care 'cause y'all niggas smilin' and shit. I fucks wit' my baby."

"Well, yo baby been fuckin' wit' T-bo," Booman said.

"Who?"

Booman sucked his teeth, making a face. "T-bo, man. You know. Be on the rap shit. Slick be dancin'. Used to fuck with that dance group, uuuh—"

"Animation," Monte finished for him. "Well, the *Show Stoppaz,* now, ever since they signed with Soulja Boy. His ad-lib stealin' ass."

"Slip-and-slide chest ass!" Booman said, laughing.

Monte and Tone burst out laughing.

Tone glanced back at his apartment door. "Aye, let me get in the house 'fo Ma Dukes start thinkin' crazy. I'ma get up wit' y'all."

"Say no moe."

"Word."

Tone dapped them up, took his suitcase in the house, and settled down. After checking his MySpace on the living room computer, he called Lauren, a girl he only broke it off with because he was being sent away. She stayed in Brook View, a nearby neighborhood. He let her know what time it was now that he was back. She was noticeably happy, but told him she would think about it.

"Yea, whatever," he said. "Don't get one of these niggas hurt."

He hung up the phone with confidence. She was fronting, and he knew it. He had her heart like she had his.

Chapter 25

Sensual moans could be heard as the clap of flesh meeting flesh reverberated throughout the room.

"You like how I'm fuckin' this pussy?" Dee-Dee said.

"Mmmm, yes," the petite Indian girl cooed. She had long jet-black hair, on which Dee-Dee tugged as he fucked her doggy-style on the bed.

There was a knock at the door, but he didn't stop. "Yo!"

"Aye, this Skeet, bra. I got a play at the church on Panhandle. Keep that bitch on ice for me."

Dee-Dee was putting on, thrusting into her hard. "I got you, bra."

"Bet!" Skeet said, laughing and running down the stairs.

The Indian girl looked back. "What you mean you got him?"

He slapped her hard on the ass. "Shut up and take this dick, bitch."

***

"That's Skeet, right there," Mickey said, pointing up the street at Skeet as he exited the trap in blue jeans, a white T-shirt, navy-blue Jordan #5's and a gold bandanna tied around his neck.

Mickey was in the backseat of Hitman's red Nissan Altima, sitting beside JT. In the front seat was Hitman who was the driver, and Razor. They had been parked curb-side three houses down, scoping out TMC's trap for the last half hour, and were ready to make their move.

JT's phone vibrated, and he answered. "Hello."

"It's prolly like six or seven more of they ass in the spot," Mickey said, continuing to give Hitman and Razor the rundown. "They strapped but the whole 12 thing gone catch 'em off guard. They gone try to dip before they shoot it out. They ain't the type of niggas to go gung-ho on the police if they can avoid it. They got shit to live for and a lot to lose, if you know what I mean."

Hitman and Razor did know what he meant. Even under the cold gray sky they could tell that Greystone was an affluent neighborhood. Like your-neighbors-would-report-you-to-the-housing-authorities-for-not-keeping-your-yard-up-to-par affluent. It was apparent by the looks of the nicely trimmed lawns, and the absence of the leaves in the yards with naked trees. Everything seemed meticulous. Even the mailboxes perched at the end of every driveway. Hitman could see a Dr. Seuss movie being shot there in the summer time.

JT clasped his flip-phone shut. "That was Wooh. He made the call. Skeet's on his was to meet him at the church up the street."

"Where's Trello?" Mickey turned back in his seat, looking out the back window.

"Just chill," Hitman said. "He comin'. All we gotta do is sit tight and make sho nobody try to run up while the lick goin' down. That includes the real police as well."

Skeet bent the corner, up ahead, and moments later, a black, unmarked Crown Vic and a silver, unmarked Dodge Charger turned into the neighborhood.

"There they go right there," Razor said.

Both vehicles pulled curbside in front of the trap, and cut their engines. The driver side door of the Crown Vic opened, and someone's hand reached up, placing a bright alternating red cone siren on the roof. It was Mecca. He got out the Vic, dressed in a Clayton County deputy uniform. Getting out on the passenger side, wearing the same thing, was Rightside.

Trello climbed out the driver side of the Charger in a forest green suit and brown dress shoes, a detective badge visibly hanging from a dog-tag chain on his neck. They had a brief huddle, then approached the door and knocked.

Elijah R. Freeman

Chapter 26

"Oww, right there," the Indian girl said, feeling her orgasm building up. "Right there."

Dee-Dee continued to hammer away at her walls, each thrust striking her spot. Downstairs he could hear someone beating on the door.

"Mmm—hmm—Cum on this dick," he said, fucking her harder. Faster. Digging deeper. Feeding her long strokes. "Make that pussy foam on this dick. Give me that shit."

"Oww, get it, daddy. Get this pussy."

Below, someone was beating on the door again.

Still stroking, Dee-Dee sucked his teeth. "Get the fuckin door, Gino!"

***

"A'ight, A'ight. Shit!" Gino finished bagging up a zip of mid, then made his way from the kitchen to the front door, bypassing two TMC affiliates playing *Mortal Kombat Versus DC Universe* on the PlayStation 3 in the living room. As he reached the door there was another knock, and Dru was climbing the stairs, smoking a blunt. He was rocking white, black and baby blue Air Maxes, some black LRG jeans, with a gold bandanna hanging out the front right pocket, and he was shirtless, leaving the handle of the black .40 tucked in his waistline exposed.

"Fuck yeen answer the door, nigga?" Gino said.

"Gone walk right pass it and shit. Lookin' and shit."

Dru shrugged and kept going. "I'm high."

"Yo mufuckin' ass ain't that high." Gino looked through the peephole and saw two deputies and a detective. "Oh, shit! 12!"

Dru turned around, panic in his eyes. "Quit playin'."

"Where the fuck they do that at? You don't cry wolf in the trap." Gino pointed at the door. "The fuckin' police out there. Go put the drugs up and put Dee-Dee on point."

Dru's high was instantly blown. He snubbed his blunt out, and ran upstairs while Gino made a dash for the kitchen.

"12!" Gino yelled to the TMC affiliates in the living room in passing. He could hear them scrambling around the living room as he tucked the zip he just bagged up down his boxer briefs.

At the sound of more beating on the front door, he rushed back to it, pausing to take a deep breath before opening it. Dru finished ducking the work off and took off to alert Dee-Dee.

Bwa! Bwa! Bwa!

"Da fuck!" He shot to the stairs but paused when, halfway down, he saw Gino laid out convulsing in a puddle of his own blood, with three bullet holes to the chest, two deputies and a detective standing over him, holding guns.

"Nooo!"

They looked up at him and opened fire immediately. He ducked and ran back up the stairs, into a room at the end of the hallway to the right, where he could see the top of the stairs, and pulled his .40 off his hip. Looking around the door frame at the staircase, he could see them advancing up the stairs minus one deputy. He snatched his head back, sweating and breathing hard, as though he had run a mile instead of the simple sprint up the stairs.

What did he do for them to shoot him? he thought. *Better yet, what the fuck did I do for them to shoot at me? What the fuck is going on?*

A door opened on the left side of the hallway and Dee-Dee stepped out. "Man, what the fuck is y'all d—"

Bwa! Bwa!

Dee-Dee fell back into the room, and the girl he had been fucking began screaming. Dru peeked around the corner just in time to see the deputy disappear into the room while the detective, gun drawn, peeked into the bathroom, flicking on the light.

"Shut the fuck up," the deputy yelled.

Bwa! Bwa!

No more screams.

The deputy ran back out the room as the detective finished searching the bathroom. Dru pulled his head back, clutching his gun to his chest, with his eyes closed. His heart pounded like that of an endangered animal, chasing out his expectations of civility and letting in the fear of anarchy and barbaric violence. Breathing through his open mouth, he made not the slightest sound. If they made any he was not certain he could hear them above his own inner drumming.

I gotta get the fuck out of here, he thought.

Thinking fast, he scanned the room for something he could use as a diversion, and decided on the light bulb next to the digital scale atop a nightstand beside an air mattress. He snatched it up and took another peek into the hallway as a bead of sweat trickled down the side of his face. Empty. Apparently, they had gone back down the stairs. No chance. He threw the light bulb into the room across from him, where it struck the wall with a loud crash.

"We got 'em, yo!" Dru heard a voice say.

He heard footsteps run across the hallway into the room, and he wasted no time. Shooting to the window, he lifted the seal and climbed out. He hopped to the balcony, shimmied down the wood structure; and, losing his grip halfway down, he fell to the ground with a thud. Coughing from the sudden inhalation of cold air, he picked himself up off the ground and couldn't believe it. The two TMC affiliates that had been slugging it out on PlayStation 3 were tied up in the living room, and a deputy was ransacking the kitchen, searching for God-knew-what.

"What the fuck is—" Dru muttered under his breath, but stopped himself from finishing the words from fear of being caught. He looked around, stumbled backwards, turned and took off through a neighbor's backyard, jumping a tall wooden fence.

***

Skeet was speed walking down Panhandle Road, coming up on the church.

I'm finna go back and fuck the shit out this hoe, he thought, looking up and down the street. He had to be on point for M.O.B 23 affiliates. The road on the side of the church was an entrance to Bonanza. It was around this area that Lil Richie had been killed.

In the church parking lot was one lone car, a green Audi. Skeet pulled out his phone and called the play back. Confirming that it was them in the green Audi, he crossed the street and approached the car. As he walked up on it, the back and driver side window rolled down, and pistols came out.

"Blatt!" someone from inside the car yelled.

Skeet turned around to run, and shots rang out behind him. He had only taken three steps when his back was riddled with bullets, leaving red spots in the back of his white T-shirt. He crumpled to the ground and Wooh hopped out, looking both ways as he jogged to his body.

"Come on, Wooh, let's get out of here," Loso yelled from the rented Audi. He opened the passenger door and stood up, watching Wooh over the roof of the car. Four cars cruised by, going up Panhandle towards Tara Road. "Wooh!"

Wooh patted Skeet down, took his phone, money and drugs, then jogged back to the Audi. Loso climbed back in as he reached the car. Wooh got in, and both of them slammed their doors. The two homies in the backseat were calling Hitman to let him know Skeet had been dealt with.

Loso looked at Wooh. "Man, you crazy as hell. You know that?"

"Naw, bra. I'm hungry." Wooh put the car in drive. "I was born hungry."

He smashed out the church parking lot, sure of two things: that one day he would be someone great, and that tomorrow morning, this incident would be all over the news.

Chapter 27

Yara sat in the back of one of her uncle's many limos as she cruised along the road headed to one of his private estates. He would have come to pick her up himself, but was busy entertaining a house full of guests who were there for one of the many parties he hosted throughout the year for his friends in politics. With her was her cocaine-white pit bull, Chica, who had been a gift from Purp two years ago on her twenty-second birthday. At the time, she resembled a ball of snow that barely filled both palms of her hands. At two weeks old she had been taken from her mother two weeks early and because of this, Yara had been left with no other choice but to feed her warm baby formula milk from a bottle as though she had gave birth to her herself. This went on for a little over a month until her teeth came in. Chica was like her own, and outside of the Benji Family she was all that Yara had left of Purp.

She wiped a tear away as the thought crossed her mind. The temperature was warm, and the clear blue sky was a reminder of the tropical West Indies weather. You definitely couldn't tell it was October, but that was Santo Domingo for you. It was never winter in the Dominican Republic; at least it never felt that way.

They pulled up to the security gate, where two Hispanic men in white long sleeve silk shirts and black slacks granted them access. The large steel gates opened and they proceeded down a long driveway until finally they reached the massive mansion, which sat off the coast of the Atlantic Ocean. Yara admired the lush greenery in the front yard of her childhood home and the elaborate fountain that sat in the center of the circular driveway. It was definitely a posh,

171

secluded dwelling. Cutting the engine, the driver got out, walked around to her door, and opened it. Yara stepped out with the most expensive pair of Jimmy Choo heels from the upcoming Spring collection gracing her feet. The driver took her hand, helping her out of the limo, and couldn't help but notice the white Chanel bandage dress she wore showed every curve of her body. Chica hopped out behind her, and the driver closed the door.

The fresh scent from the ocean was like heaven as she took a deep inhale through her nostrils, and the moist air journeyed to her lungs. The sounds of the waves traveling through the air to her ears as they crashed onto the shore was so relaxing, as was the cool breeze.

The driver told her in Spanish he would get her luggage and she thanked him in the same language.

Well, here goes nothing, she thought as she entered her uncle's home, passing under the security cameras with Chica on her heels.

***

"Can I have your attention everyone?" Eduardo spoke in broken English to the crowd of people scattered about the stone structure of his back porch. In the middle of the porch was a large in-ground swimming pool, beside which he stood in a white cotton short sleeve button down, holding up a Champagne flute. In his early fifties, he was a mid-height Hispanic man with a hard lined face, a square chin covered with a salt and pepper beard, and wavy jet-black hair that stopped at his shoulders.

The crowd grew quiet and he continued, the view of the endless ocean a beautiful backdrop behind him.

"I would like to propose a toast. To our campaign accountant, and my longtime friend, Jose' Martinez. Jose!"

Everyone clapped as a short fair-skinned man with greasy black hair stepped forth, smiling in a casual cream suit and loafers. He shook Eduardo's hand and embraced him. They pulled apart and the guest quieted.

Eduardo was all smiles. "Anything you would like to say?"

Jose' chuckled. "No, my friend. It is an honor on my behalf to be of assistance to such good people."

The guest "awed" and clapped once again, and Eduardo signaled for one of the many butlers present. A nimble butler approached, beating the others to it, bearing a silver tray with a single Champagne flute, and Jose' grabbed it. The crowd began to settle.

Eduardo raised his glass. "To Jose'."

"To Jose'," the guests said in unison.

Just as everyone went to down their drinks, Eduardo's smiled transformed to a scowl and he smashed his Champagne flute to the ground.

"*Hijo de la chingada*," he yelled, pointing at Jose'.

The butler from whom Jose' had grabbed his Champagne flute flipped the silver tray, snatched a .38 revolver from underneath and put it to Jose's head in a flash. The guests gasped in shock and began to murmur.

Three Dominican goons moved through the crowd from the right and left, the front man of each trio toting an AK-47, until they reached Jose'.

"Eduardo, my friend," Jose' yelled, pure fear etched in his face as two goons took hold of him from each side, and he found himself under the barrel of three deadly weapons. "What is going on? What is this?"

"So you thought I wouldn't learn of your treason?" Eduardo said. "Oso!"

A huge, stocky Dominican with short dark hair came forth from the crowd, handed Eduardo a jagged edge machete and stood by, his deadly grimace locked on Jose'.

Jose' began to sweat. "Eduardo!"

"Jose' here has been stealing from campaign funds," he said, pointing the machete at him. "From us! Investing the money into the United States stock market."

"No-no-no, Eduardo, wait. I can explain," Jose' pleaded. "I was not stealing. I was simply trying to grow the account, eh? For everyone's benefit. Not just mine. I swear!"

Eduardo shook his head. "You wretched snake. Even when he is caught dead to the wrong, he still lies. There is no slithering out of this one. I've been watching the account since you began stealing over a year ago and not one penny has been returned despite the fact that your accounts, in and outside the country continue to grow."

"But I—"

"Silence!" Eduardo yelled. "You disgust me." He turned to the crowd. "No treason of any kind will be tolerated amongst this familia. The act is unforgivable. The punishment is death. Open him up!"

Yara stepped out onto the balcony overlooking the porch and watched as two of the henchmen took hold of each of Jose's feet, and they wrestled him to the ground. The crowd looked on in horror as he struggled to no avail, pleading for dear life until finally, he was stretched out in an 'X'. One goon holding down each of his forearms, the other goons pinning down his ankles.

Eduardo walked around to stand over the top part of Jose's body. "This is the price of betrayal!"

He raised the machete high over his head and brought it down on Jose's wrist, severing it completely and staining the stone with dark crimson blood. Jose' released a blood curdling scream, and some guests turned their heads, realizing that this was not something they were prepared to see, but not Yara. She hadn't blinked an eye, and watched on as her uncle brought the machete down on Jose's other wrist, dismembering his hand as he struggled on in vain. Blood was gushing from his wounds, staining the stone red. Eduardo walked around to his lower half letting out a stream of curse words in Spanish. The crowd was in shock.

"No, Eduardo! Please!" Jose tried to sit up with all the strength he could muster, but was pushed backed to the ground by his shoulders. "I beg you. I—"

Ching!

"Arrrgh!" Jose' cried out in anguish, feeling his foot chopped off. A wet mark appeared in the crotch area of his slacks and grew as he pissed on himself. His other foot was twitching as though it knew what was to come.

Eduardo pointed the machete at Jose' once more. "No more will your feet make haste to deception. You're washed up." Eduardo raised the machete up over his shoulder.

Jose's eyes grew wide, and he shook his head vigorously. "No-no-no. Aaaargh!"

Eduardo chopped off his other foot. "Toss the thief for a swim."

The goons lifted Jose' from the ground and tossed him into the swimming pool, turning the water a murky red as his blood mixed. The crowd was struck with terror as they watched Jose' splash and flail about in the pool attempting to swim, but with no hands or feet it was pointless. He fought with everything he had to stay above the surface, kicking and wailing as he choked on water, until his movements slowed, stopped, and he floated face down in the pool.

Eduardo turned to face his guest. "Let this be a message to anyone who even thinks of crossing this fam—" His words trailed off when he looked up and locked eyes with Yara. He smiled. "Family."

***

The ocean waves washed ashore as Yara and Eduardo walked barefoot across the soft white sand, leaving indents of their trail as they went. Beside them, the entire coastline was clear, and as the sun set in the horizon they spoke in peace.

"Some party, eh?"

"Tell me about it," Yara said.

"I apologize for you having to see that. I wasn't expecting you so early."

Yara released a heavy sigh. "No need. I understand, completely. Besides, you and I both know I've seen worse. Nothing new to me."

"And I apologize for that as well." Eduardo shook his head. "I never wanted to expose you to this lifestyle. I wanted better, as I knew your mother would've wanted. My baby sister would've wanted for her daughter what she always longed for herself. To get an education. But mama and papa were simple people. A farmer and a carpenter who could not afford to give her that chance. But I made a way." Eduardo stopped walking, and looked down at Yara who stopped as well. "She died before she could fulfill her dreams, so I made it my business to raise you the best I could

176

and see to it that you were given that chance. I sent you to America for school but—"

"That wasn't my dream," Yara said. "It was my mother's."

Eduardo smiled as his eyes welled up with tears. "I know." He dropped his head, nodded, then started walking again, Yara continuing along his side. "So what brings you home? Trouble in the States again?"

"Not this time. At least not with the Feds."

"Local police?"

Yara shook her head. "No, nothing like that. E—" she paused, taking a breath and exhaling. She was fighting back tears as she steeled herself for what she was about to say. "Emanuel was killed."

Alarmed, Eduardo stopped her, grabbing her shoulder. "He's dead?"

Yara nodded, wiping away a falling tear.

"Are you in danger of any kind?"

Yara shook her head. "No. But, I need your help."

Eduardo's brow creased, looking her in the eye with all seriousness. "Anything."

"I need a plug, Uncle. I want to take over the Benji Family, and I need some leverage. I have a—"

"No," Eduardo walked on.

Yara was on his heels. "But Uncle, Emanuel and I, we built that empire together. It's as much as mine as it was his."

"I do not care. I will not help you bury yourself. This is not the life for you, Yara."

Yara caught him by the shoulder, making him face her. "But it's the one I'm living. The one I've been living all along. Open your eyes, Uncle. I'm not the little girl that arrived on your doorstep with the yellow dress anymore. I am a drug Queen who wants her crown, and with or without you, I am going to get it."

Eduardo stared her down, and Yara held his gaze, knowing without a shadow of a doubt he could see the fire within them. She was dead serious, and if the eyes were indeed the road to the soul, she wanted him to see that she was far from bullshiting. She meant business. There was no point in trying to talk her out of it. Anyone who thought they could were wasting their breath. She hadn't flown all this way on the strength. Her mind was set in stone, and with the loss of Purp, so was her heart. Besides, it was in her, not on her. She couldn't just un-become someone she had grown to be. The Benji Family was rightfully hers, and she wasn't about to let anyone take it from her. They stood for a moment in silence as the breeze blew against their clothes. Streaks of clouds lined the sky, and behind them, the sun resembled a pinkish-orange half sphere of fire that appeared to be going into the ocean as it set.

"Your mother would've never wanted this for you."

Yara didn't respond, and at that, Eduardo looked away at the distant waves headed to shore.

"Oso goes with you."

"Deal."

"I do not like this, Yara."

"I know."

"I am not happy with your decision; nevertheless, I have no choice but to respect it. You are stubborn. Just like—"

"My mother," Yara said, cutting him off.

"No." Eduardo smiled, facing her again. "That you may have picked up from me."

They shared a laugh and continued their stroll, talking of Yara's plans and crunching numbers until—before they knew it—the night had crept up on them and they decided to take it in.

Hours later she retired for sleep in her old bedroom and had a dream in which she talked to Purp.

"*The world is ours,*" he said.

Elijah R. Freeman

Chapter 28

"Where the fuck this nigga at?" Huncho threw a vase at the wall, shattering it on impact. He pointed at TD. "I'm tellin' you, he up to something."

TD shook his head. He was seated on the long couch beside Trill Gottem. Longway sat on the couch adjacent to them, with Diesel Gottem sitting on the arm rest. Together, including Huncho, they made up the group that would be responsible for governing 2DM's affairs: The Elect.

All members of The Elect were present except for Rock and D-Day. Considering D-Day was in chain-gang, his absence was excused. He had a phone but couldn't pull it out his duck-off spot until after inspection hours, or risk getting caught with it.

"That shit with Champ," Huncho continued. "Any idea who was behind it?"

Everyone looked around the room at each other, shrugging.

"No?" Huncho made a face shrugging "Not one clue?"

"You think Rock?" Trill said. "He's all about standing behind his word and this movement. Buck a treaty? That ain't e'en lil bra stilo."

"Neither is changing his number and fallin' off the face of the Earth, but ain't nan nigga in this room heard shit from him. Niggas who also believe in standing behind their word and this movement." Huncho exhaled, taking the edge off. "I ain't takin' shots at the Dub, bra. At a time like this, the last thing we need is division amongst us. We don't' want to show any dissension in the heat of this thing either. All I'm saying is that since the weeks following Thugga's death, Rock ain't been the same."

"Who would be?" Trill said.

"You ever lost your brother?" Diesel asked. "Your real brother."

"A'ight. Huncho closed his eyes, and put his hands up in surrender. "Y'all right. Maybe he just needs time to get his head together."

Huncho really didn't believe the words that came out his mouth, even as he said them. He had expected that reaction from Trill and Diesel. Not just because Rock was an original 2-Dub affiliate, nor because he was Flame's blood cousin. Everyone loved Rock, even he himself. He just couldn't ignore the signs, or lie to himself, for that matter. They hadn't seen the look in Rock's eyes that day in the Aquatic Center parking lot. In them, Huncho had seen a demon, one he had only seen before in the eyes of Dre. But seeing that he was fighting a losing battle, he changed the subject to their common enemy.

"Anyone got a lead on the whereabouts of these Blood niggas yet?" Huncho cleared his throat. "These Billy Blood niggas."

"None at Riverdale High," Diesel said. "Not Billy. Couple Piru's, a few G-Shine Bloods, but that's it."

Huncho looked from face to face. "Nobody else?"

"Hell naw." Trill shook his head. "I been tryna hold the trap together."

"Well, it just got easier," Huncho said.

Trill's brow creased. "Hell you tawmbout?"

"We back plugged in. We meet the connect this weekend." Huncho grinned. "I've been in contact with Ricardo."

Trill looked unsure. "And you trust him? He could be workin' a mean one."

"This man had Carlos, his blood brother and his family, knocked off for tryna implicate me and Purp in a conspiracy. Fuckin' right I trust him. Besides, he ain't lookin' at nearly as much time as he was before."

Diesel was looking as though he had missed something. "Before?"

"Before the evidence and witness list dwindled to nearly nothing." Huncho waved it off. "Long story short, he finna take a ten-year plea in Federal court sometime soon, and when he does, we'll be movin' most of the Cartel's product."

"That's 'bout the best news I done heard all year," Diesel said. "Right behind the fact that we finna have a black president."

Longway raised a finger and spoke up for the first time. "Any of y'all remember Brando?"

Huncho nodded. "Yea, his flexin' ass called me from the County earlier this year. Put me on game about Nard and Mel. What about him?"

Everyone turned, facing Longway.

"Copped out to two years and went down the road. Called me last night a few hours after the prison Chaplain called Ma Dukes to tell her 'bout Dumbway. He was at the same prison." Longway paused, a distant look in his eyes. "Saw the whole thing. Said it fucked him up. Told me he was coming out the chow-hall when three Blood niggas stabbed him up. Red-Rag, Slime, and another one who he didn't recognize."

A tear escaped his eye, and he wiped it away quickly. If anyone noticed, they didn't show it.

"Anyways, I told him about them supposed to be having money on yo head and beef with the Mafia, and he said he would nonchalantly ask around and find us some type of ups on them.

Huncho was stuck. "Now, that's the best news I done heard. Think he can pull it off?"

Longway shrugged. "I don't know. He from the hood, so he is a Frontstreet nigga. He be flexin' and shit, but he looked up to Dumbway back in the G, so who knows? Guess we'll find out eventually."

"He will." TD was nodding slowly. "Trust me."

"Yea," Trill said. "If nothin' else, they'll tell him what he wants to know to get him the fuck out they face."

Everyone laughed to that. They ended the meeting, deciding to change the location of The Spot for the second time that year, just to be on the safe side. The last thing any of them wanted was a replay of 2005 when Hit Squad Taliban caught them slippin'. It had cost Ski his life, and they had no intentions of losing any more Mafiosos to war. Not if they could help it. They packed everything up, leaving Diesel in charge of seeing to it that it all made it to storage.

Huncho pulled off from Frontstreet, kicking himself for freezing up. He was supposed to have told Trill that he was leaving him and TD the plug because he was falling back from the game.

Damn!

On the way home, D-Day hit his line. He filled him in on what was said at the meeting, and gave him the names of the Bloods responsible for Dumbway's murder, telling him to see what he could find out about what the Billy's had going on in the streets.

Back in Villa Rica, Camry had just finished burping Justin and putting him to sleep. Making her way to the kitchen to fix Zakayla a peanut butter and jelly sandwich, she looked at the *Fossil* watch gracing her wrist. She was wondering where Huncho was, and if he would overcome the streets before the lifestyle took him under for good.

The End

Submission Guideline

Submit the first three chapters of your completed manuscript to ldpsubmissions@gmail.com, subject line: Your book's title. The manuscript must be in a .doc file and sent as an attachment. Document should be in Times New Roman, double spaced and in size 12 font. Also, provide your synopsis and full contact information. If sending multiple submissions, they must each be in a separate email.

Have a story but no way to send it electronically? You can still submit to LDP/Ca$h Presents. Send in the first three chapters, written or typed, of your completed manuscript to:

LDP: Submissions Dept
Po Box 944
Stockbridge, Ga 30281

DO NOT send original manuscript. Must be a duplicate.

Provide your synopsis and a cover letter containing your full contact information.

Thanks for considering LDP and Ca$h Presents.

Coming Soon from Lock Down Publications/Ca$h Presents

BOW DOWN TO MY GANGSTA

By **Ca$h**

TORN BETWEEN TWO

By **Coffee**

THE STREETS STAINED MY SOUL **II**

By **Marcellus Allen**

BLOOD OF A BOSS **VI**

SHADOWS OF THE GAME II

By **Askari**

LOYAL TO THE GAME **IV**

By **T.J. & Jelissa**

A DOPEBOY'S PRAYER **II**

By **Eddie "Wolf" Lee**

IF LOVING YOU IS WRONG... **III**

By **Jelissa**

TRUE SAVAGE **VII**

MIDNIGHT CARTEL III

DOPE BOY MAGIC IV

By **Chris Green**

BLAST FOR ME **III**

A SAVAGE DOPEBOY III

CUTTHROAT MAFIA II

By **Ghost**

A HUSTLER'S DECEIT III

KILL ZONE **II**

Elijah R. Freeman

BAE BELONGS TO ME III
A DOPE BOY'S QUEEN II
By **Aryanna**
COKE KINGS V
KING OF THE TRAP II
By **T.J. Edwards**
GORILLAZ IN THE BAY V
De'Kari
THE STREETS ARE CALLING II
Duquie Wilson
KINGPIN KILLAZ IV
STREET KINGS III
PAID IN BLOOD III
CARTEL KILLAZ IV
DOPE GODS II
Hood Rich
SINS OF A HUSTLA II
ASAD
KINGZ OF THE GAME V
Playa Ray
SLAUGHTER GANG IV
RUTHLESS HEART IV
By Willie Slaughter
THE HEART OF A SAVAGE III
By Jibril Williams
FUK SHYT II
By Blakk Diamond

188

FEAR MY GANGSTA 5

THE REALEST KILLAS

By Tranay Adams

TRAP GOD II

By Troublesome

YAYO IV

A SHOOTER'S AMBITION III

By S. Allen

GHOST MOB

Stilloan Robinson

KINGPIN DREAMS III

By Paper Boi Rari

CREAM

By Yolanda Moore

SON OF A DOPE FIEND II

By Renta

FOREVER GANGSTA II

GLOCKS ON SATIN SHEETS II

By Adrian Dulan

LOYALTY AIN'T PROMISED II

By Keith Williams

THE PRICE YOU PAY FOR LOVE II

DOPE GIRL MAGIC III

By Destiny Skai

CONFESSIONS OF A GANGSTA II

By Nicholas Lock

I'M NOTHING WITHOUT HIS LOVE II

Elijah R. Freeman

By Monet Dragun
CAUGHT UP IN THE LIFE III
By Robert Baptiste
LIFE OF A SAVAGE IV
A GANGSTA'S QUR'AN II
By **Romell Tukes**
QUIET MONEY III
By **Trai'Quan**
THE STREETS MADE ME II
By **Larry D. Wright**
THE ULTIMATE SACRIFICE VI
IF YOU CROSSM ME ONCE II
By **Anthony Fields**
THE LIFE OF A HOOD STAR
By Ca$h & Rashia Wilson

Available Now

RESTRAINING ORDER **I & II**
By **CA$H & Coffee**
LOVE KNOWS NO BOUNDARIES **I II & III**
By **Coffee**
RAISED AS A GOON I, II, III & IV
BRED BY THE SLUMS I, II, III
BLAST FOR ME I & II

ROTTEN TO THE CORE I II III

A BRONX TALE I, II, III

DUFFEL BAG CARTEL I II III IV

HEARTLESS GOON I II III IV

A SAVAGE DOPEBOY I II

HEARTLESS GOON I II III

DRUG LORDS I II III

CUTTHROAT MAFIA

By **Ghost**

LAY IT DOWN **I & II**

LAST OF A DYING BREED

BLOOD STAINS OF A SHOTTA I & II III

By **Jamaica**

LOYAL TO THE GAME I II III

LIFE OF SIN I, II III

By **TJ & Jelissa**

BLOODY COMMAS I & II

SKI MASK CARTEL I II & III

KING OF NEW YORK I II,III IV V

RISE TO POWER I II III

COKE KINGS I II III IV

BORN HEARTLESS I II III IV

KING OF THE TRAP

By **T.J. Edwards**

IF LOVING HIM IS WRONG…I & II

LOVE ME EVEN WHEN IT HURTS I II III

By **Jelissa**

Elijah R. Freeman

WHEN THE STREETS CLAP BACK I & II III

THE HEART OF A SAVAGE I II

By **Jibril Williams**

A DISTINGUISHED THUG STOLE MY HEART I II & III

LOVE SHOULDN'T HURT I II III IV

RENEGADE BOYS I II III IV

PAID IN KARMA I II III

By **Meesha**

A GANGSTER'S CODE I &, II III

A GANGSTER'S SYN I II III

THE SAVAGE LIFE I II III

CHAINED TO THE STREETS I II III

By **J-Blunt**

PUSH IT TO THE LIMIT

By **Bre' Hayes**

BLOOD OF A BOSS **I, II, III, IV, V**

SHADOWS OF THE GAME

By **Askari**

THE STREETS BLEED MURDER **I, II & III**

THE HEART OF A GANGSTA I II& III

By **Jerry Jackson**

CUM FOR ME I II III IV V

An **LDP Erotica Collaboration**

BRIDE OF A HUSTLA **I II & II**

THE FETTI GIRLS **I, II& III**

CORRUPTED BY A GANGSTA I, II III, IV

BLINDED BY HIS LOVE

THE PRICE YOU PAY FOR LOVE

DOPE GIRL MAGIC I II

By **Destiny Skai**

WHEN A GOOD GIRL GOES BAD

By **Adrienne**

THE COST OF LOYALTY I II III

By Kweli

A GANGSTER'S REVENGE **I II III & IV**

THE BOSS MAN'S DAUGHTERS I II III IV V

A SAVAGE LOVE **I & II**

BAE BELONGS TO ME I II

A HUSTLER'S DECEIT I, II, III

WHAT BAD BITCHES DO I, II, III

SOUL OF A MONSTER I II III

KILL ZONE

A DOPE BOY'S QUEEN

By **Aryanna**

A KINGPIN'S AMBITON

A KINGPIN'S AMBITION **II**

I MURDER FOR THE DOUGH

By **Ambitious**

TRUE SAVAGE I II III IV V VI

DOPE BOY MAGIC I, II, III

MIDNIGHT CARTEL I II

By **Chris Green**

A DOPEBOY'S PRAYER

By **Eddie "Wolf" Lee**

Elijah R. Freeman

THE KING CARTEL **I, II & III**

By **Frank Gresham**

THESE NIGGAS AIN'T LOYAL **I, II & III**

By **Nikki Tee**

GANGSTA SHYT **I II &III**

By **CATO**

THE ULTIMATE BETRAYAL

By **Phoenix**

BOSS'N UP **I , II & III**

By **Royal Nicole**

I LOVE YOU TO DEATH

By Destiny J

I RIDE FOR MY HITTA

I STILL RIDE FOR MY HITTA

By **Misty Holt**

LOVE & CHASIN' PAPER

By **Qay Crockett**

TO DIE IN VAIN

SINS OF A HUSTLA

By **ASAD**

BROOKLYN HUSTLAZ

By **Boogsy Morina**

BROOKLYN ON LOCK I & II

By **Sonovia**

GANGSTA CITY

By **Teddy Duke**

A DRUG KING AND HIS DIAMOND I & II III

Triggadale 3

A DOPEMAN'S RICHES

HER MAN, MINE'S TOO I, II

CASH MONEY HO'S

By Nicole Goosby

TRAPHOUSE KING **I II & III**

KINGPIN KILLAZ I II III

STREET KINGS I II

PAID IN BLOOD **I II**

CARTEL KILLAZ I II III

DOPE GODS

By **Hood Rich**

LIPSTICK KILLAH **I, II, III**

CRIME OF PASSION I II & III

By **Mimi**

STEADY MOBBN' **I, II, III**

THE STREETS STAINED MY SOUL

By **Marcellus Allen**

WHO SHOT YA **I, II, III**

SON OF A DOPE FIEND

Renta

GORILLAZ IN THE BAY **I II III IV**

TEARS OF A GANGSTA I II

DE'KARI

TRIGGADALE I II III

Elijah R. Freeman

GOD BLESS THE TRAPPERS I, II, III

THESE SCANDALOUS STREETS I, II, III

Elijah R. Freeman

FEAR MY GANGSTA I, II, III IV

THESE STREETS DON'T LOVE NOBODY I, II

BURY ME A G I, II, III, IV, V

A GANGSTA'S EMPIRE I, II, III, IV

THE DOPEMAN'S BODYGAURD I II

Tranay Adams

THE STREETS ARE CALLING

Duquie Wilson

MARRIED TO A BOSS... I II III

By Destiny Skai & Chris Green

KINGZ OF THE GAME I II III IV

Playa Ray

SLAUGHTER GANG I II III

RUTHLESS HEART I II III

By Willie Slaughter

FUK SHYT

By Blakk Diamond

DON'T F#CK WITH MY HEART I II

By Linnea

ADDICTED TO THE DRAMA I II III

By Jamila

YAYO I II III

A SHOOTER'S AMBITION I II

By S. Allen

TRAP GOD

By Troublesome

FOREVER GANGSTA

GLOCKS ON SATIN SHEETS

By Adrian Dulan

TOE TAGZ I II III

By Ah'Million

KINGPIN DREAMS I II

By Paper Boi Rari

CONFESSIONS OF A GANGSTA

By Nicholas Lock

I'M NOTHING WITHOUT HIS LOVE

By Monet Dragun

CAUGHT UP IN THE LIFE I II

By Robert Baptiste

NEW TO THE GAME I II III

By **Malik D. Rice**

LIFE OF A SAVAGE I II III

A GANGSTA'S QUR'AN

By **Romell Tukes**

LOYALTY AIN'T PROMISED

By Keith Williams

QUIET MONEY I II

By **Trai'Quan**

THE STREETS MADE ME

By **Larry D. Wright**

THE ULTIMATE SACRIFICE I, II, III, IV, V

KHADIFI

IF YOU CROSS ME ONCE

By **Anthony Fields**

Elijah R. Freeman

THE LIFE OF A HOOD STAR
By Ca$h & Rashia Wilson

BOOKS BY LDP'S CEO, CA$H

TRUST IN NO MAN

TRUST IN NO MAN 2

TRUST IN NO MAN 3

BONDED BY BLOOD

SHORTY GOT A THUG

THUGS CRY

THUGS CRY 2

THUGS CRY 3

TRUST NO BITCH

TRUST NO BITCH 2

TRUST NO BITCH 3

TIL MY CASKET DROPS

RESTRAINING ORDER

RESTRAINING ORDER 2

IN LOVE WITH A CONVICT

LIFE OF A HOOD STAR

Coming Soon

BONDED BY BLOOD 2

BOW DOWN TO MY GANGSTA

Elijah R. Freeman

CPSIA information can be obtained
at www.ICGtesting.com
Printed in the USA
FSHW022254191021
85588FS